Power Riches Or Death (PROD)
Vol. III

Power Riches Or Death (PROD) Vol. III, Never Beg or Bow
© 2025, by Charles Flagg

Hardcopy ISBN: 979-8-9923201-2-1
Ebook ISBN: 979-8-9923201-3-8

Published by Regal Rhythms Poetry LLC
Printed in the United States of America

Edited by: Regal Rhythms Poetry LLC
Cover Art: Adam Hayden

Acknowledgements

I thank everyone who supported me throughout this life changing dream making process.

TABLE OF CONTENTS

Chapter 1 1

Chapter 2 8

Chapter 3 13

Chapter 4 18

Chapter 5 25

Chapter 6 29

Chapter 7 31

Chapter 8 34

Chapter 9 37

Chapter 10 45

Chapter 11 56

Chapter 12 61

Chapter 13 68

Chapter 14 77

Chapter 15 96

Chapter 16 103

Chapter 17 112

Chapter 18 125

Chapter 19 130

Chapter 20 147

Chapter 1

Ms. Private Eye didn't have a clue where to find Isis until she located me with her. This should be a real interesting time. Where was she hiding? If she was a snake, she could have bitten me.

"Hey Isis, that was my friend Angie that just texted. She is on her way over here. Do you mind if she joins us?" I asked.

"No, not at all. I get this booth to kind of have room for my thoughts to breathe, while I take in the energy and enjoy the atmosphere," she confided.

Barely able to hear her over the laughs, that dude was up there killing it. Tall slinky with big lips, he kinda' reminded me of JJ from Good Times, but you can tell he spoke from experience and wasn't just telling jokes.

"How do you like the show so far Isis?" She slowly edged her way closer to me like she was trying to whisper the answer in my ear. I couldn't help but notice the intense smell of mint and dark chocolate being even stronger while staring at the words as they floated over her shiny lips.

"The show is fine so far. That guy up there now is really doing his thang. He reminds me of that one guy by the lips," she said, searching for his name.

"Who JJ?" I blurted while clapping my hands.

"I was going to say his real name, but I can't think of it right now," she pondered momentarily.

"Me either. It's on the tip of my tongue."

"I wish I was on the tip of your tongue, spinning around like a disco ball!" She confessed slowly moving closer. Somewhere in another world, the needle on the record scratched putting a halt to even the thought of spinning disco balls.

"Excuse me. I didn't interrupt anything did I?" Angie butted in. My honorary Craft men had been sippin' a little. The gloss in her eyes revealed that truth and the small orange stain on her shirt let me know she'd been snacking too.

"Naw. We're talking about the show," I said. "Angie, this is Isis. Isis this is Angie." It was tension from the beginning. The pleasantries out of the way Angie grabbed the champagne bottle popped the top, as if it is easier to ask for forgiveness than it is to ask for permission. She sat to the left of me, finally resting her tired feet.

"Sorry. I don't mean to be rude, but do you mind?" Angie spoke directly into Isis' direction while she poured a glass of bubbly.

"No, I don't mind. Help yourself," Isis said as non-confrontational as possible.

"I'm so used to being in V.I.P. with my girls. We just grab bottles and pop them. It was looking so good in that ice, sweating like a WHORE in church." Angie put heavy emphasis on whore.

"No problem. Drink up. Have as much as you want," Isis insisted.

"I ain't gonna drink too much. I gotta keep an eye on you two," she said jokingly despite telling the truth. Angie paused then looked towards the stage before turning her attention back to us. "That nigga up there looking like Jimmie Walker is funny as hell."

Yeah, that's his name." Me and Isis said in unison like twins.

"Yawl sound like kissing cousins." The words spoken by my drunken sidekick

3

warranted no response. She figured as much and continued with her prodding, "So Isis, how did you and Craft meet?"

"We met through a friend of mines name Fresh I knew from college. He felt Craft was someone I could link up with to help promote my pieces."

"Promote your pieces, huh? A piece of this and a piece of that I bet," Angie replied sarcastically.

Feeling the energy shift, this was the perfect time to intervene. "Hey Angie, chill. Me and Isis's relationship is strictly business." As soon as those words left my mouth, Isis rubbed on my thigh under the table, trying to make the situation hard and awkward with a big emphasis on the word HARD.

Despite being about two jokes into his routine, Angie slurred judgingly, "The guy up there now isn't even funny. I could do better than that." Angie P.I. thought. That was the queue Isis needed to get rid of my partner in crime.

"Angie, you know you can sign up and try your own routine if you like." The push that she needed was from a stranger trying to jack me off under the table.

"I don't know. I got to keep my eyes on you two," she repeated again.

"That's nonsense. He is in good hands with me," she emphasized while squeezing and massaging me gently under the table. "The signup sheet is over there. You might be able to go on next." Was Isis really trying to get Angie to find her calling, or trying to get her to call it quits. Either way, she was trying to get her away from us.

"Hey Angie, you been drinking. You don't have to go up there. You can chill," I said, trying to be the voice of reason and stop Isis from finishing up the hand job that felt so good. The boldness increased the quality of my response to her off rhythm stroking hand.

"I'm going up there. Where is the signup sheet?" Angie left in search of her calling, barefoot, champagne glass in one hand and champagne bottle in the other.

"I hope your friend does well up there. The stage can be a frightening thing." Isis said.

"I don't know why she went up there drunk." Liquid courage wasn't the reason Isis was being so bold. I don't know if she had been celibate or selling a bit. But Isis was trying to rub a nut out.

5

"Have you ever gotten your dick sucked at a comedy show before?" Her lips, glossy. Her mouth watery like she was starving to taste me. Unable to remove her hand, her firm grip was locked on me. Her eyes said don't move, peace be still. Ducking under the table, she began to taste me slowly. My feet were balling like fist in my shoes. Chiseling on me with her tongue, she sculpted whatever she wanted to create. Like hardwood, she molded me, tasted me, and consumed me. Taking what she wanted from me, and I didn't want to do anything but comply with her.

Maybe this is what that last comedian's weed was supposed to make him feel like. Like you're touching stars. Like taking what you want is the only way you can really get it. Stunned that she caught me off guard. Seduced. Beaten in my own game, but I still wouldn't have played it any other way. This is what husbands wished they got after a hard day of work instead of contempt. This was that I appreciate you type of head without asking.

Isis was cleaning up the spill she caused to overflow with her mouth. Angie was taking the stage, nervous, alcohol in tow getting ready to look like a genius or a fool. I wondered if I should record it or not. What the hell, I gotta record it.

"You're gonna video record your friend making a fool out of herself?"

"Hey, some people like to eat nuts at comedy clubs and some people like to be nuts at comedy clubs. Pun intended. To each their own."

Chapter 2

Angie: "Test 1,2.....Testing 1,2 and....3. How many people in a relationship...by a show of hands?...Don't get to barking and making wolf sounds...I can tell by them side burns you like to howl at the moon with your little dick ass...Them shoes look like a size zero...It's true the shoe size thing don't mean nothing...but I couldn't fuck with no short little feet nigga no matter how big his dick is...I'd rather have a tall nigga that need to put a sock in his grey sweats before I mess with a short man...," the crowd roared as Angie continued.

"I don't like short men...They are too controlling...I had one that like to sit outside of the bathroom door when I was trying to use the toilet...The bathroom didn't even have a window...Did that nigga think I had somebody hiding under the sink...I'm like damn, can I use the bathroom in peace? ....Ladies I know yawl done had a possessive man before...Nigga hiding clothes so you can't go out with your girls talking about I don't know where your outfit went...This one nigga couldn't keep a job, cause' he stayed leaving work to drive by my house...He want to talk on the phone his whole shift to make sure I didn't go nowhere...You can't be broke and stalkish, that math ain't mathin'....... I might put up with it from a nigga with money, but a broke nigga hell no!...I ain't got the patience to be ya momma and ya woman nigga...Help me pay some bills, fuck that!...That shit will wear you out...I'm telling you.......Have you stressing...Have your hair falling out, losing weight, cause' you can't eat," Angie said.

"I know that's right," shouted a lady in the audience.

Angie continued, "I've been there before too... This is from experience... Got people thinking you smoking some dope or got AIDS or something...It will have you eating bad and gaining weight too... ... Ahhh! As she drank straight from the champagne bottle.......That hit the spot...Anyway what was I saying?... .....All this ass, I like to eat...I like a man that can cook...But I like cooking for my man too...I thought filling his stomach and emptying his nuts would keep him from cheating....advice from my momma, but why did I listen....

SHAKING MY MUTHAFUCKIN'
HEAD.......... She could never keep a man...I
don't know if it was her pussy or her cookin....
Anyway my last nigga end up finding him a
bitch who like to cook and empty his
balls...Eventually we was sharing a nigga who
stomach got bigger, but his dick got smaller..
Hey why yawl turn the mic off? I was just
warming up...I couldn't find the sign-up
sheet.....that nasal voice nerd back there tried
to set me up."

People turned towards the back looking at
everyone who had booths in the rear of the
venue. Due to the darkness of the place, we
couldn't be singled out. Angie was helped off
the stage and besides the meltdown, she did
good I thought. She handled it like they used to
play the dozens at the lunchroom table in high
school. No letterman jacket for me, just
skippin' school and getting girls.

"That Angie is a wild one. She doesn't hold
her liquor very well. I think you should drop
her off, so we can continue our night, Mr.
Naughty man." She placed her hand once again
on my thigh. "I like sucking your dick, Craft. I
like the way it pulsates in my mouth. It fits so
snug. Makes it more challenging to breathe out

of my nose." She took a sip out of her glass and continued her sells pitch. "I like the way your warmness goes down my throat. I came twice just by tasting you. I loved sucking it so much. There is more in store, if you come back to my place," Isis promised.

"I got business to handle tonight. I won't be able to make it Isis. Maybe, next time," I tried to let her down easy.

"BULLSHIT! After you forced me to suck your dick, you are coming with me."

"What the fuck you talking about? I didn't force you to do shit. You volunteered to suck my dick," I reminded her.

"We'll see who they believe," she threatened.

"Bitch, you better quit playing with me."

"What seems to be the problem? Does this bitch have a problem, boss?" Angie's words were slightly slurred as she made her way to the scene of the fake news.

"Huh, bitch?" Angie said. "What's going on here?" Out of nowhere, she grabbed Isis by her well-attached ponytail. Usually, I'm the man of peace, but this bitch needs to get dealt with. Angie pounded her head into the table knocking over the ice bucket. Isis grabbed the plastic champagne flute splashing the contents in Angie's face, but that didn't do nothing but piss her off. Her medium size hands formed nice size fists. By the movements of her hands, you could tell she grew up around the boxing gym. Isis was dazed on her way to sleepy land when I moved in like a ref who had seen enough to stop the fight. Angie was like post jail Tyson; she wasn't going to stop her shark frenzy until she bit her ear off. I was finally able to peel her off Isis, her once nicely attached ponytail was now a trophy held tightly as spoils of war.

Chapter 3

We were escorted out of the venue by a couple of muscle-bound giants that we continued to fight against. The melee traveled outside past the gatekeeper who nearly denied me access.

"I want my hundred dollars back!" Angie yelled at the man she bribed. "Give me my hundred dollars! I want my money." Standing there in shock from her allegations, he denied them every step of the way.

"You didn't give me no money, lady. You're drunk. I work for everything I got. I can't afford to lose my job. We ain't allowed to take tips," he continued speaking to anyone who'd listen. Angie wanted a refund, and I wanted to get the fuck up out of there.

"Angie, come on girl. Fuck it!" I yelled.

You guys better not come back on the premises, or I will be calling the cops," the baritone voiced bouncer advised us.

This time no beating on my chest bombarding my way through the door. I walked away nearly dragging Angie trying to keep her from falling. Now she is the defiant one. "Fuck it!" I picked her up, carrying her to the passenger side of the truck. She kicked her legs as her last act to break free losing a shoe in the process.

"Be your ass still before we get hit by one of these cars," I commanded as we weaved through the traffic like the fabric of life. I stood Angie up to her feet and leaned her up against the truck.

"Where is my other shoe. My foot is cold on this nasty ground," she complained. I peeped her glass slipper being reduced to shreds by the tires of speeding cars. "Those wings wasn't all the way done," she said before a slurry of buffalo chunks and ranch juice splashed up against her front wheel. She wiped her mouth with her hand before continuing sharing her thoughts. "Fuck love, fuck love!" she repeated a few more times before passing out on the passenger side.

"I should take a picture of your extra ass. This don't make no sense." My watch was sprinkled with small specks of saliva and whatever else. It was getting late. We were supposed to meet the cop at the hospital. Plus, I wanted to check on Ice anyway. The phone rang and it was Unc. I didn't want to answer. I wasn't trying to hear shit he had to say now.

"Hello. What's up Unc?" I paused dramatically before my sporadic breathing.

"Did I catch you at a bad time?"

"Naw, not at all," I said while trying to keep an eye on Angie."

"Your place going up in flames has made national news. There was a headless body found. Do you know if it was Church or not?" Unc questioned.

Just hearing his name had me angry that I wasn't there. "I was told by my source that it is possibly Dick, my agent and lawyer. He has this ring he wears, and they said the body was that of a white male."

"So where is Church?"

"He's dead," I said painfully.

"I know he's dead nephew. Where is his body?" he inquired. I paused speechless at the reality of my ignorance. Unc continued, "How do you not know where the body is?"

"I'm working on it," I fired back.

"Working on it?" he doubted. "You call running around town with that woman working on it? With Turtle's sister? The man who cut you out of millions. How can you trust her?"

15

he lectured. "She benefits from your fall as well."

"She has helped me get some pieces off of the board," I reminded him.

"Yes, nephew, but in doing so, you are keeping her on the board. You are going to make her reign instead of using her for what she is, a pawn. You are giving her too much value and power. Are you trying to make her a king?" he questioned.

"Why would I make her King?"

"The better question is why didn't you dispose of her already? She is a liability. You are a man with many instant infatuations."

"I have had my eye on Angie. She has done a hell of a job getting me information and driving me around," I corrected him.

"She is a driver. Give her a chauffeur's hat and uniform, and allow her to do her job. Anything beyond that scope is a disaster waiting to happen. Your father always put pussy on a pedestal too. Look where it got him," he said, infuriating me.

"Leave my father out of it. You old sick miserable muthafucka!" I said sternly.

"Look at that. I done touched a nerve. You better clean this shit up or my miserable ass will be your company," Unc threatened.

I hung up on that muthafucka. He never wanna' listen. Like damn, you ain't right all the fucking time. It's more than one way to get something done. If Angie ass was working for the other side, I will deal with her ass as severely as possible.   At the end of the day, it was very necessary for the Isis situation to be handled like that. False accusations have ruined lives since the beginning of time. The fact that she would try that with me was very surprising despite me now being at a point in life where nothing surprises me. The aggressor and willing participant played the victim.

Chapter 4

I pulled into the hospital's parking lot located in the rear of the building, but still facing a small but high traffic street. The meeting spot was on the first floor. This time of night, the parking spaces are plentiful. Parked the truck with Angie still in it, close to a spot that was well lit for dark places. Grabbed Angie's phone and ducked behind one of the few cars that were still parked. It was a perfect view of the entrance. Plus, we still had about 15 minutes until the meeting time. The traffic was speeding by, and The Diamond King was playing in damn near every car that passed. He will be mourned until the next big things come along tomorrow. I didn't have any luck cracking Angie's code on her phone. I thought I learned a few skills from Stormy, cause' she used to stay figuring out my password. I will still be able to answer it when the cop calls before he pulls up to say he's late or otherwise.

The passenger side door flew open, and Angie came tumbling out shouting, "Craft, where you at? Why my mouth taste so nasty?"

I was still ducking down hiding like she was the enemy. "I heard my song playing in my sleep. I thought it was coming from my phone." Finally, I revealed myself from the shadows like a kid playing tag. Her phone clutched conspicuously in my hand as if I was the one who found it. "What you doing with my phone? You look like the type of nigga that will go through phones, hide them and then say you found it." Stumbling and still drunk, she tried to audition her stage show in the middle of the parking lot.

"Girl, your drunk ass is crazy! You damn near killed Isis when you put them paws on her like that," I said playfully.

"Shit! I thought I was dreaming. No wonder I got strands of hair in my mouth. I thought you tried something while I was sleep," she slurred.

"Girl, cut that shit out! One false accusation is enough for a lifetime."

"I'm sorry. I got a lot on my mind and that girl was just rubbing me the wrong way," she confessed.

"Shit, you came over there ready to square up with her from the very start," I reminded.

"I was, but it wasn't her personally……"
she revealed before pausing to take a deep
breath. She cleared her sinuses with a big glob
of snot flying out of her mouth and onto the
blacktop. Then she continued, "It wasn't
personal. My ex called on the phone in the
middle of me eyeing Isis talking about he's
thinking about moving my son in with him
permanently. This was just supposed to be
until Jr. got his act together. I'm not giving up
my son. He's all I got."

"Angie, if Jr. staying with his father on a
permanent basis will help him mature and
grow better, then what's the problem," I asked.

"Because he can do all of that with me. I
can raise my son to be a great man. He just
wants to compete with me, cause' I left his ass
and didn't look back."

"Whatever yawl decide, I just hope it's the
best for the child and yawl don't let egos,
pride, and shit get in the way," I warned.

"You ain't got no kids with your selfish ass.
I know that bitch sucked your dick. Your ass is
trifflin' like that," she angrily accused.

"Girl, you drunk. Go back in the truck and
wait for your cop dude to call," I demanded.

"I was going to go back in the truck until you told me too. I ain't going nowhere now," Angie protested angrily.

Giving in I replied, "Well, lean your vomit smelling ass on this car without setting the alarm off."

She thought about going back to the truck instead, but I think those few feet away must have looked like miles. She leaned on the car that I was originally kneeling near and began to sob silently. I could hear pain in her tears.

"Angie, chill! Everything will be ok. You got to trust me," I assured her.

"I'm done trusting men. That's all yawl do is lie. I'm a great mother and I deserve to raise my son into the perfect man," she preached.

"Shhh. Calm down. We got to pay attention before we get killed and your ex will be raising your son alone for real."

"No, the fuck he ain't ! I'm staying alive to raise my son."

"Angie, text your homeboy. He is definitely late now, even with the CP time grace period. You know this nigga late," I told her.

She said, "I will call him. You always like texting. Calling is more personable than texting."

"That's all you do is text me eggplant emojis and smiley faces. What the hell you talking about?" I argued.

"That's personal and not business. This is business and not personal. Know the difference," Angie countered.

"Just call that nigga with your stanky breath ass," I said.

"You would still let me suck it," she replied jokingly.

"Shid. I got options. I ain't hardly pressed. Plus, yo shit just decent with good breath. I know that funky shit can't make it no better." The phone began to ring, but I could hear it ringing in the garage. The sound was coming from a nearby location like the cop beat us here. "Angie, you hear that."

"Hear what?" she asked.

"The phone ringing," I whispered.

"Yeah, I hear it. I'm calling him ain't I?" she stated.

"No, not that. The phone is in the garage with us. SHHHH. Just listen," I said even lower. Her eyes were the only clue that revealed that she heard it. Fear soon glowed in her eyes like my Uncle's halos.

"Oh my god. I hope ain't nothing wrong. No one picked up. His voicemail is full," she said, pressing redial just in case the second time would charm him out of hiding. This time she walked and stumbled towards the sound. "His car is over there. That's where the sound is coming from."

The reddish Caddy was parked at an angle taking up two parking spaces. I don't know if he was in a hurry or wanted the extra room.

"Don't touch shit Angie. We don't need no dead cop on our hands!" I yelled.

"We ain't killed no cop," she replied.

"I knoooow.... but if that nigga over there dead that mean people can make it look like we did it." His phone was in the car. I got close trying not to trigger an alarm or explosion. I peered through the smoke tinted windows with my hands on my forehead like a visor. "He ain't in there," I announced with a confused look on my face.

"Are you sure? Let me see," she said, bending over to look.

"Girl, move your ass out the way. I ain't touching no doors or nothing."

"What if he is in the trunk and needs our help?" she insisted.

"If he in that muthafuckan trunk somebody else gonna be helping him and it ain't gonna be us!" I yelled, pacing back and forth. I wore the sole out on my shoes. I looked down. I could see a little splash of blood from the melee between Isis and Angie. It was weird. This is how the murder detective must have felt when he looked at his shoe knowing that he was cleverly displaying a murder trophy in public.

Chapter 5

"Excuse me. Can we help you find your floor?" said one of the two hospital security officers who drove around in a golf cart trying to look official. The tall fat one was driving, and the slender one spoke on his walkie-talkie to base. The radio reflected in the lenses of his mirrored frames.

"We are looking to visit my wife, Shanice Mitchell. I think we may have come to the wrong lot," I answered quickly.

"Dispatch, is there a patient by the name of Shanice Mitchell?" The slender guy looked like he took his job seriously. His heavily creased pants were tucked inside of his freshly polished black military boots. He was the muscle, and the fat guy was the voice.

"While my partner checks on the status of the patient, would you mind showing us some I.D.?" Any other day I would of talked shit, and gave them a hard time. But I didn't want shit to be in that trunk: a body, a bomb, or some dope. Fuck that!

"Yeah, I got my I.D. right here sir," I said respectfully as possible.

"Ma'am, what about your I.D.?" he turned to look at Angie. I knew she was finna' amp up. I gave her a friendly nudge just to remind her of the seriousness of what could be if we got caught up in this shit with this missing cop.

"Yeah, there is a patient by that name, but the visiting hours are over," he informed us while spitting what had to be tobacco juice on to the concrete, splashing on the tip of his boot. Smiling at the blemish amongst the shine, he wiped it with his hand.

"Look Bear. I got myself with some of this snuff juice," he laughed between words.

"Here is my license, sir. I thought I left it in my truck, but it was in my back pocket," she said.

"DeeDee Kim? What's your relationship to the patient?" he pressed. Who the fuck is DeeDee Kim, I thought to myself? That name sounds Chinese as fuck. She gave me a what the fuck I'm looking at look.

"I'm the roommate of the patient. We are all life partners," she lied quickly.

"Yawl do that ménage a whatchamacallit? My wife said if I be good, we might do one for my birthday," he said, grinning from ear to ear.

"Oh, shut up, dummy. Your wife barely sucks your dick on your birthday," Bear said. I guess Bear was the mouth and the alpha between the two.

"Bear, you know I hate when you call me dumb," he said sadly handing us back our I.D.'s

"Sorry for my partner, folks. The elevators are over that way," he directed pointing us towards the word ELEVATOR in big red letters. We waited until they screeched off down the other end of the dark and dimly lit parking lot with their radios crackling as they investigated other suspicious folk.

"Craft, let's go back to the car and see what we can find out," Angie insisted.

"Don't let that private investigator shit go to your head. I'm going upstairs to check on Ice. You can play in the dark by your damn self, Mrs. Kim."

"It's Miss Kim. I ain't found a man who can handle all of this wild and tender love," she boasted.

"That name sounds like you give five da'wa sucky sucky," I said in my best Chinese accent.

"This sucky sucky is worth way more than five dollars, nigga. This elevator needs to hurry

27

up. I got to tinkle!" she hollered while squirming around.

"Your ass ain't tinkled in damn near 40 years. Just don't piss in the corner with your wild ass," I demanded.

"Oh hush. This is an I.D. Tags made for me. This was back when we was cool. Before he got all thirsty and cutthroat with his lying janky ass," she recalled.

"Let me see what it looks like," She handed over the license proudly like she was showing off her report card with all A's. "Hawaii! Your ass probably never even been to Hawaii."

"I have your nosey ass know that my passport got stamps all over it, Lil Baby: from cruises to girls trips. You know Hawaii is just a hop and a skip."

"My girl can't go on no all-girl trip," I said.

"Why not?" she asked.

"Cause yawl don't do nothing but be chasing dick, and trying to get yawl groove back," I insinuated.

"If she gotta go somewhere to get her groove back, who fault is that?" she snapped.

I gave a rebuttal, "Whoever she is fucking, I guess. But it wouldn't be me, so it wouldn't matter."

Chapter 6

The door to the elevator finally came down to the lower level. A mixed couple holding hands walked out. The man came through with his head up looking straight ahead. The woman walked out looking in my direction. Thick for a white girl, she had that look like she only fuck with niggas. That look that might have broken her father's heart when he first found out. But with thighs and ass like that, that's a brother's speed all day long.

"That's a cute couple. Have you ever dealt with a white girl before?" she questioned.

"I have female acquaintances of many races. The closest I have come to dealing with an Asian female is you, Miss Kim. I thought that pussy would be slanted and sideways. "Ha-ha!"

"Yeah right. I'm more than just a pussy. I'm highly sexual, but I am very particular too. I went hard like that with you, mainly because I always wanted to feel you inside of me. It was just something about you not trying to get on with me like my brother's other friends. You just kept everything cool and treated me

29

with so much love and respect that I just wanted to test it," she exposed.

"Test it?" I questioned. Then she continued, "Yeah, test that thang to see what that hype was about."

"Shid, ain't no hype over here. It's an acquired taste," I flirted. "Nigga that shit taste worse than my breath right now. Every time I talk, I got to stop myself from throwing up," Angie said.

"It still ain't stop your nasty mouth ass from talking," I said with my hand partly over my mouth. This time the lady wearing the bun in her hair wasn't there. It was empty on that floor. A cart from housekeeping wasn't being watched by anyone.

"That cleaner the hospital be using is strong as hell. My one girl used to be getting that for us all the time, but she got fired for sleeping on the job. I don't know how people work third shift," Angie continued. "That shit is for the birds."

Chapter 7

I wasn't paying Angie ass no attention at all. I was trying to remember how to get back to the room. I think it was 5317. This day had been so wild that I was forgetting simple shit.

"You don't remember where to go do you?" she asked.

"Yeah, I know where I'm going. Follow me. It's room 5317."

"Ok cool, but the lower 5300's is that way," she corrected.

"I knew that. Was testing you," I joked.

"Why don't guys like asking for directions? My daddy used to get lost all of the time when we had family trips."

"Girl, give your mouth a rest, so I can concentrate."

"How much concentration does it take to follow some numbers in bold colors."

"Angie, shut it!" I demanded.

Finally, motor mouth rested her jaws for more than a second. Now, I could see where I'm going. "Shit, I missed a turn somewhere," I huffed.

"I was going to say something, but you said you knew where you was going, and my talking obviously stopped you from concentrating."

"Angie, you ain't got to be that damn petty," I interrupted.

"I got a license that say Petty LaBelle too, so don't come for me unless I send for you," she warned.

"Yeah, that's original. I just noticed you got slides on your feet."

"Yeah, I lost my other shoe somewhere near the comedy spot," she answered, looking down at her feet.

We walked up to room 5317. The same nurse that wanted to pray for me was there, but this time her eyes weren't as inviting. Her demeanor was kind of stand offish.

"Hey. How are you doing?" I said, trying to get her attention.

"Good, Mr. Craft. Ms. Mitchell is awake. The medication had her groggy, but she has been speaking with the police for the last half an hour. They told us to contact them as soon as she was able to speak," she updated me.

"I wanted someone to contact me," I complained.

"Sir, law enforcement gets priority over family."

"I bet they do," I admitted.

"This is between me and you, but they are asking her questions about a dock heist that they think she is involved in. They wanted to cuff her to the bed, but the younger cop talked the older gentlemen out of it," she explained.

"Thanks for the info. I appreciate it."

"What the police talking to your friend for? Shit. I ain't trying to be funny. Ever since I started working with you, it ain't been shit but police around everywhere we go."

"Yeah, you a secret agent or undercover?" I reminded my stanky breath companion.

"Boy, I might fuck one, but I don't fuck with them like that. This one I had he used to trick big time," she thought aloud. I looked at her eyes like didn't you just say that you was selective and all that shit.

"Don't be looking at me like that. That was back before I was saved and shit……Psalms 45:6. Yes, Lord," she waved her hand.

"Girl, bring your loud ass on," I commanded.

Chapter 8

"Mr. Craft, I'm glad you can join us. We were just wrapping up our little talk with Shanice here. She gave us some very helpful information." Angie gave me a little nudge and head movement to let me know that the cop we were supposed to meet was the guy in uniform with the murder detective. Sgt. Jones was our contact, and I didn't know what to make of him. But we weren't all on the same page as the Three Stooges going through their routine.

"Detective Corral, you must be the hardest working guy on the force. You are just everywhere today," I said.

"I'm the hardest working guy on the Special Investigation force, he corrected. Sgt. Jones is really the guy who gets a lot done. He is like my eyes when I'm not around," he said.

I nudged Angie, "We gotta watch your boy. He might be one of them," I suggested.

"Sgt. Jones, this is Mr. Craft. You might need to keep an eye on him. This slick mother fucker's name came up originally in the investigation, but he was ruled out early on. However, Shanice here will need to be questioned more thoroughly. After she is released in a few days, I want her to come down to the station and finish this interview," he requested.

"I didn't have nothing to do with any of this. I'm just here with my friend to visit his friend," Angie informed. Angie felt guilty or just had her mouth closed for too long. Either way, all eyes were on her now. Even Shanice rolled her eyes at me.

"Your taste in women has quite a range. Where did you find this garbage mouth broad from? The odor alone should humble her enough to keep that dick hole shut," the murder detective said angrily.

"Chill out with that shit, Corral. Don't be disrespecting her," I said, speaking up for my garbage mouth friend.

"Naw, I don't need you to speak up for me, nigga. I don't care if you are a cop or not; you don't talk to me like that," Angie slurred.

His look was intense, and his pupils were dilated. The whites of his eyes were almost black. Sgt. Jones went to shut the door completely. Corral looked down at his shoe and grinned, snapping out of his deep dark trance. "Bitch, I will speak to you however the fuck I please! If I feel like tossing your wide booty ass out of that fucking window, I will do so. That ghetto shit is cool with these niggas you surround yourself with, but bitch listen closely. I will come to your home, put my pistol in your fucking mouth, and blow your brains all over the fucking wall," he promised.

"Hey man, what the fuck wrong with you? Don't talk to her like that and don't be disrespecting her period," I said, walking up to the murder detective.

"Hey Detective. Let's not lose our cool here. It's late and people are tired. We'll be in touch folks. Enjoy the rest of your evening," Sergeant friendly ass finally said. I see he didn't say too much. Angie was teary-eyed, but quiet. I turned to watch them walk out of the door, knowing that Corral had to be removed as well. If I could get him and Tags together that would be the perfect storm.

"Angie, are you ok?" I comforted her.

"Yeah, I'm fine. That sick ass nigga is something else. You can see the maniac in his eyes. He believes that shit he be talking," Angie said, biting her lip.

Chapter 9

I walked over to Ice, propped up, and asked, "Hey Baby, how are you doing."

"I'm fine. My dad and mom just left. They were arguing as usual. They just can't get along. She still won't forgive him and move on with her life. Even though I'm the one in the hospital, she still managed to make it about her." Angie, gazed out of the window, no doubt she was thinking about those words.

"Hey Angie. Come over here and let me introduce you to my best friend Ice," I insisted. She ignored me and remained in her zone. Ice tapped my hand signaling me to leave her alone. The rain poured down hitting the windowsill. She didn't move a bit, as if her mind was somewhere safe or somewhere she enjoyed more. Me and Ice were not invited.

"I dreamed about you a lot. Detective what's his face brought you up early. He said that you were questioned about the heist originally and said that anything I could provide for him would be greatly appreciated. I told him about Tags and Ira beating me up, and that I don't know nothing about no heist. I said

Ira worked with me, but our relationship was platonic and professional even though he wanted more. I didn't really know Tags beyond what I learned from you, but I didn't tell him that," she brought me up to speed.

"Did he mention my place being torched?"

"He said that a body was found in it without a head."

"Yeah, that body might be Dick's, and Church's body is around here somewhere without a head as well," I said.

"Oh My God! Hopefully, Church isn't dead. We didn't get along all that well when he drank, but I still wouldn't wish that on anyone," she said.

"No, it's official. Church is dead. Tags had his head in a box. I seen it with my own eyes," I said, dropping my head.

"No! I'm sorry to hear that. I was hoping it was just a rumor." Concerned, I said, "Enough about me. How are you holding up?"

"I am doing a lot better than I look. That is for sure. I fought my ass off to look like this. Damnit, it was well worth it."

"Them scars will be beauty marks, baby," I tried to console her.

"It's too late to be running all that game this way. I was very upset with you before this happened. You was so textbook. I thought you would switch up just a little. But you played that we won't speak unless she reaches out to me shit to a T." I thought we were better than that. I thought for a moment you would look past, being the one always in control. That you would cater to me with just a phone call that you wouldn't do for anyone else but me!"

"Ice, it ain't even like that," I moved closer.

"That's exactly how it is. I'm lying in this bed, and I couldn't get my mind off you. The way that you smell. The way that you feel. The way your eyes look like the color of new copper when the sun hits them just right."

"Don't be like that. I thought about you as well. I was hurt that I didn't defend you. That I wasn't there. I wished I would have opened the door and stopped them," I said sadly.

"Being who you are saved your life. They were waiting for you to come in and use your key. I tried to scream the first time, but Ira put his big hand over my mouth. I bit him with all my might, and he rewarded me with a blow to the jaw filled with nothing but the hate that he used to love me with. If he had hit me directly, he would have broken my jaw. Luckily, I was able to get knocked out from the graze of his fist," she regretfully told me.

"Damn, baby. I'm so sorry," I comforted her while sitting on the edge of the bed holding her like I never wanted to let her go. Like forever wasn't temporary, and our season would never end. Tight, but gentle. Kissing her on her chapped lips that were usually soft and sweet.

"Yeah, I know my lips are chapped. I'm down right now, but I'm not out," Ice said with confidence.

"You definitely not out, baby. We're finna' rule the world."

"Craft, you know the world is your dream. I just want you. But since that's what you want baby, we can rule it together," she said.

"Sorry to break up this reunion, but for us to rule the world together it's a must that we get the Detective off the fucking board. He isn't going to let any of us rest, and that bitch of a Sergeant was supposed to be my contact. I got some choice words for his soft ass," Angie said angrily.

"Angie, that talk is for a small group in a small room," I said.

"Boss, this is the perfect size group in the perfect size room." Angie walked around pacing deep in thought as if she was trying to mastermind the assassination of the detective.

"Angie, have a seat and relax your mind," I said, pointing to the chair with extra hospital blankets partially covering it.

"I'm fine. I just need to get me some air. I'm going to go for a drive. It always helps me clear my head," she reminded me.

I voiced my concern, "Hey Angie. Just walk this one off, if you need a breather. You've been drinking, and I don't want you to hurt yourself."

"I appreciate the thought, but I got this. You're preoccupied trying to rekindle your love with Ice. Excuse me, I mean Shanice," Angie said with an air of disdain.

"Hey, Ice. Give us a minute," I said, motioning Angie to follow me out to the waiting area. She was hesitant at first, then she reluctantly followed me.

"Nice meeting you, Shanice. I wish it was on better terms," Angie said.

"Likewise, Angie," Ice replied dryly.

I grabbed her shoulder to get a feel of her vibe. She didn't jerk away or tell me to stop, so

I knew she just wanted to talk. "Angie, I need you use your beautiful mind in this situation. We can't allow our emotions to get us into a place that would eventually prevent us from doing what needs to be done."

She turned to me somber, no quick-witted jokes, just eyes filled with tears overflowing onto her face. "It just hurts…I'm hurt…The way he talked to me wasn't called for. My contact didn't do anything in terms of defending me. He just stood there ready to follow any order that fucking monster was going to give him," Angie said.

"Baby, you know I got your back. It ain't nothing going to happen to you, period," I assured her.

"It ain't about you having my back. I know you gonna have Ice's back before you have mines. You ain't even got to interrupt me with one of your lies. I did a lot for you, Craft. Mainly, because I wanted too. I know I talk too much sometimes. I just was trying to break the monotony. The room seemed so depressing like we were visiting someone on their deathbed," Angie confessed.

I hugged her tight, not even caring about the dried vomit and food stains on her clothes. I needed to reassure her that we were on one accord, and that we are going to see the mission all the way through, no matter what my death bed patient uncle said. "Everything will be fine. Promise me you'll be safe. Go ahead and head home, so you can freshen up and get a nap in. Call me once you get in the house, and don't leave out until I call you to come get me."

"Yessa, Boss," she said as her sarcasm was resurrected.

"That's what I'm talking about. Pick your spirits up. Lift that big head up and walk like you know you're the shit," I encouraged her.

"Boy, my head ain't hardly big. It might just be my hairstyle."

"Girl, you ain't got enough hair. That's mostly head." She looked at me with eyes like she wanted to fling cusswords my way. Instead, she didn't. She caught me off guard.

"I love you, Craft. I've always loved you. You ain't gotta say it back. I know your love is going to be rekindled for that woman lying in that hospital," she said with envy.

I stood speechless for a moment knowing that she was right. Do you want me to walk you down?" I asked.

"No, I got it from here." She left dignified with her head held high.

Chapter 10

Back in the room, Ice was sitting up all the way like she was going somewhere. The light from the lamp closest to her offered some light to the dimly lit room. The get well soon balloons and the stuffed bear that held them sat slightly illuminated.

"Why you sitting up, instead of lying down and resting your body? " I asked, thinking of his well-being.

She replied, "I'm sitting up to let you know that I was listening. It seems Angie thinks she has a permanent place in our lives and that isn't true at all."

"What do you mean a permanent place?"

"I heard her tell you that she loves you."

"Damn, she didn't even say it that loud. How you hear her," I responded, surprised.

"It was loud enough. Besides, I don't like her. She doesn't think before she speaks. She just likes to run off at the mouth, because she is starved for attention," Ice scolded.

"Angie is cool peoples. She didn't mean any harm."

"She didn't have to. Her lack of couth made this temporary room hostile. All she had to do was speak when spoken to at the most. We don't need a fucking court jester," she continued.

I looked over at Ice who rarely even used cuss words. While looking in her eyes, I could see that she was exhausted. Those chapped lips still looked kissable. "You think I took this ass whoopin' protecting you, so I could be replaced by a woman like that. Hell, naw. I gave myself to you, because I want you to know that I want to be completely yours. I know you fucked her. I can tell how clingy she is with you. Putting her life on the line, cause' she is dickmotized," Ice accused.

"Chill out with all of those accusations." I said quickly.

"Accusations?" Her head snapped back as if she had been waiting on that response. "What have I accused you of that was a lie? Haven't you slept with her? Didn't she say that she loves you?" she contested.

"If you know all of that, then you should know that I didn't say I love her back even though I have love for her."

46

"You do love her though. You love her mystery and her quirkiness. The way she is unpredictable," she revealed.

"You trippin. I love her as a friend. I've known her for years," I said, trying to convince her.

"Did you or did you not fuck her?" she scolded, demanding an answer.

I must have been silent for too long. She interrupted, "It's a yes or no question; don't tell me you don't remember."

I hesitantly confessed, "Yeah, wc did."

"Thank you! Was it before or after I gave myself to you?" she interrogated.

"What's with all of these questions?" I asked with my guard up.

"You ain't shit! You couldn't even wait to see if I was going to die!" she hollered.

"It wasn't even like that," I said, trying to calm her down.

"What was it like then?"

"Look, I did it to get back at Turtle for some shit he did to me," I admitted.

Instantly disgusted, she put her bandaged face into her scarred and wrapped hands and began to cry uncontrollably. "You're so childish! Don't you fucking touch me! Don't be consoling me like you do her. I'm not going to be crying over your ass for years unable to move on like my mother. She is still trapped in a time capsule! Still wearing her ring! Still buying his favorite cologne just so she can spray her sheets with it when the mood hits her. He still comes by every now and then to do who knows what knowing they will never be an item again."

I gestured to wrap my arms around her. She fought me off like I was making unwanted advances. "I'm not your father."

"I know you're not, but sometimes I think there are similar qualities that keep me drawn to you. Similar qualities that I share with my mother that keep me waiting on you. When we had sex for the first time, I thought you would instantly change, but you still maintained your poker face," Ice said, heartbroken.

"You just said me being me saved my life….Which is it?" I asked trying to weave through the confusion.

"The reality is I wish you would have came through the door and died with me, if necessary. I was scared and frightened and all I thought about is you being ok. I would have died in that apartment protecting you," she said, making me feel guilty.

"Ice…Shanice. You know damn well I would have killed anything in there to protect you. Your thoughts are coming from a dark place that has nothing to do with the truth about me," I said, defending my honor.

"The truth about you? Nigga, I can sum you up in a few words. You are a selfish, greedy, arrogant….," she attempted to ramble on.

I grabbed and hugged her until she stopped fighting, until my actions caused her to feel what my words couldn't say. Hopefully, the hugs would turn those truths into lies, because they cut me deep. I threw in the towel. Her words were like a mirror revealing a reflection that I was unwilling to see. I consoled her, rocked her, and even kissed her chapped lips that cut me every time I did so.

"Excuse me. I hope I'm not interrupting anything," said the politically correct words that came from a man wearing a white lab coat as he casually walked in without a courtesy knock. "I'm Doctor Napier, but you can call me Jack." He extended his hand to shake mines before sanitizing them at the small sink in the room." I shook his hand to be polite, but I

49

sanitized my hand with the same sanitizer that he could have used. I don't like hospitals or germs.

"You're a germophobe, but you like fucking raw. I just don't get you," Ice said on a rare rampage. I just ignored her, turning my attention towards Dr. Pissy Hands.

"So, Dr. Jack, what's the news on my lovely lady here."

"Oh, so now I'm your lady. Then that bitch gotta go. I am not playing second fiddle to her. Even if I was into threesomes, which I'm not, she definitely wouldn't be my type," she said inappropriately in front of the doctor.

I gave her that look like I had halos in my eyes spinning to get her to cooperate. "My apologies, sir. We are both very tired. What's the good news?"

"Are you guys sure you don't want me to come back a little later?" he asked looking down at his chart waiting on our response. We both ignored him, and he continued. "Well, it looks like some old scar tissue opened up during surgery. It was most likely do to the strain on your body from the assault. We have removed most of the scarring and sealed up the area that had been compromised."

"When do I get to take her home?" I interrupted.

"I'm not going home with you. We are going to my place where you can wait on me hand and foot until I am up and running," she demanded.

I gave her the look like we used to get when we asked for something in the store after we were already told we weren't getting anything.

"She will be able to go home in the next two to three days depending on how well her body takes to the medication. So far everything is looking good given the circumstances," Dr. Jack explained.

"That's definitely good news. We needed that today. Thanks Doc."

"Ms. Mitchell, if you need anything, don't hesitate to contact a nurse by pushing this button here," he instructed while pointing at the red button on the remote connected to the bed.

"I won't. Thanks again. I just can't wait to get out of here. I need to be around open windows and peaceful sounds. This machine and this T.V. is just getting on my last nerve,"

Ice complained. I rubbed her legs loving how the small hairs on her legs tickled my fingers.

"This is just temporary, Ms. Mitchel. As soon as you are well enough, you will return to your regular activities. I just need you to be patient. Outside isn't going anywhere, but you might if you rush the process," he said just as his name was called on the intercom. The specialist was needed elsewhere.

"That's me. I gotta run. You guys be kind to one another. It will help with the healing," he said, but his words sounded routine. His concern almost robotic as he went from room to room offering false hope to people that were willing to buy it, cause' insurance won't cover it.

"That doctor seemed kind of smug to me. He's fairly young, but you can tell he is very routine," Ice analyzed.

"You think everyone is routine right about now Ice," I rebutted.

"Don't tell me you didn't pick up on it."

"I did. I just ain't gonna make a big deal out of it," I replied nonchalantly.

"Oh, so I'm making a big deal out of things, because I'm sharing my concerns with you," she said, having mood swings like a chick I used to date in high school. She was pregnant, but we later found out it wasn't mines. "Yada! Yada! Ya!"

"You over there zoned out, and I'm crying out for you. I'm gonna really need you when I get out of here. I know you gonna have nurses and stuff for me, but I'mma need you with me every step of the way," she nagged.

"I will be there as much as possible. Other than high priority business, I will be making sure you are back on your feet."

"I'm going to hold you to that. It's going to feel good being wrapped in your arms listening to your heartbeat while eating something salty and sweet watching one of our throwback movies," she said, envisioning every moment.

"I can't wait until you are out of this hospital, cause' I'm tired of them lips being so chapped. They cut me every time I kiss on you," I teased.

"They are thorns protecting my rosebuds. I know you would have sex with me in this hospital room if you could."

"I would cause' I love you, not because that's all I see you for." I really meant it.

"Ira tried to get me to believe that you didn't love me. That I was just a piece of meat you were trying to use for notches on your headboard or belt…something like that. He never believed that we hadn't been intimate before. When he came over, he could smell the intimacy and the love in the air," Ice explained.

"So, what happened? How did things go from sugar to shit?"

"He didn't like the fact that I see a kingdom with you, and not just someone calling themselves king. You are a man of action. He wanted me to be more than I ever wanted to be with him. I just looked at him as a friend, but I could see how much he disliked our relationship," she revealed.

"I always thought he was a cool nigga though. I never thought he would be into the shit he was into," I said, shaking my head.

"The only reason I found out is, because Tags came to the door after we had been in there arguing. I guess he heard me through my window, or he was waiting in the hallway I'm not sure. I do know that he wanted to kill me, and Tags sat back and tried to help him. I tried to slice his fucking face in half with that chess piece. I wanted somebody to know I fought with every bit of energy I had in me," Ice detailed as tears formed when her emotions took over. Flashbacks had her stuck in the moment not able to fast forward.

I comforted her saying, "Calm down, baby. You don't need to get all worked up. Ira is gone and Tags is next."

"You make sure Tags is definitely finished. He hates you more than Ira. You helped him with so many business ventures, and he betrayed you like that," Ice reminded me.

"You just get some rest. I will take care of the situations outside of this room," I vowed her.

"It's hard for me to sit back knowing that you are out there, and everyone is against you. I'm sorry how I reacted about Angie. I can tell she loves you just by the things that she does for you. When I get out of here, I will invite her over for dinner, or something to get to know her. Maybe I can see what it is that you see in her," she admitted.

"Don't be trying to interrogate her. She is good peoples, and she has shown her value to us in this high stress situation," I reminded her.

Chapter 11

I laid in the hospital bed with Ice to comfort her and rocked her back to sleep. A few nurses came in during my visit. They checked on her to make sure she was good. I remember when big momma was in the hospital when I was a kid, she would always let me have her apple juice. That shit doesn't taste nothing like how I remembered it. Angie was en route to the hospital to get me. My days were running together so much that I don't know what day of the week it was. I needed to get out of this hospital and breathe some fresh air. I could feel where Ice was coming from. Being cooped up in this dungeon for this long can't be a good thing. No wonder people die before ever getting well.

Outside the air wasn't fresh, but it was damn sure better than the stale air coming from the air conditioning unit. Combine that with those industrial strength cleaners that they used to keep the place sanitized. Buses were rushing to get people to their destinations. People were holding up traffic texting at green lights. Horns honked, cusswords flew, a beautiful morning like this was better than lying in the hospital any day. Angie had really been a blessing driving me around, because I haven't had road rage in days, and it felt kind of good.

"Good morning brother. You got a single you can spare," said the suited stranger. Back in his day, he probably was a ladies man. A pimp maybe, but now he was the shell of the man that he once was. He was dressed in a suit from many moons ago, but his shoes had a shine to them as if he was out hustling and not homeless. "Young blood, can you hear me? Snap out of it!" He snapped his fingers as if breaking the spell of the hypnosis.

"Yeah, I hear ya, old school. What you need again?" I asked coming out of a slight daydream.

"I need a single, but I will appreciate anything but a three dolla' bill," he said, failing at his attempt to make a joke.

"You look like you got more money than me," I said jokingly.

"Just cause I'm broke, don't mean I gotta dress my worst. I still got faith in me and the almighty…Whatever you going through, young blood, remember to keep your head up," he preached. He was reminiscent of the king rising. He was a globetrotting preacher man collecting offerings and spreading his wisdom. I hadn't decided on whether I was going to give him a few dollars, so he could leave, or just enjoy the show.

"It was a time when I hustled harder and bartered before I ever had to borrow a dollar. I didn't deal with losing well. I sulked in my losses more than I appreciated my victories, until there were no more victories to celebrate. Life comes at you fast sometimes. I would rather plan than not, but I would also rather fail without a plan than be too scared to try," he continued his sermon.

"Is that part of your hustle? Is selling game part of your routine?" I said annoyed.

"Youngblood, you standing out in front of a hospital. Your eyes got heavy bags and you're pacing back and forth. I just came to offer some words of encouragement, because your day looked like it was starting off wrong, or finishing up wrong," he admitted.

I wondered what type of old dude I would be, dressing my age or trying to dress young. Angie blasting music took me out of my zone. I had to focus. I had too many thoughts racing in my mind. "I hear you old school. That's my ride. I gotta run," I responded handing him a five-dollar bill and a crumbled single.

"Hey Pretty Tony," Angie hollered through the window barely turning the music down.

"Who calling a player by his throwback name?" said the suited stranger. The still recognizable pimp/player put his hand over his forehead like a visor to assist him in recognizing the face of the voice who shouted out his name. "Who that be," he asked walking over to the truck to get a clearer picture. While I headed to the passenger side.

"It's Angie, Brenda's daughter," she responded.

"Brenda who? Awww shoot. Not Lil Angie...Girl step out of the truck, so Uncle Tony can see you girl." Angie stepped out in vibrant eye-popping colors. Her multi-color yoga pants accented that ass so well. The cashmere Lap Kiss sweatshirt looked great with it. That girl knows she can dress and get down in that kitchen for sure. "Lil Angie, I remember you, girl. You all grown up looking just like your momma. How is your momma doing?" he inquired.

"She is doing great. She had to do chemo treatments a year ago, but she bounced back once she started eating raw foods and stop doing the chemo."

"Praise God for that. You tell her Tony said hello, and that I'm glad she doing well.

"I definitely will, Tony," Angie assured him.

"You got something that I can add with this lil bit your friend gave me," said the wise man turned ingrate.

Angie reached under her armrest to grab a ten-dollar bill. Uncle Tony snuck another look at her yoga pants. "Here you go, Tony?"

"Thank you, baby girl. She gave me a ten and you gave me six. That's my momma's birthday. I'mma have to play that number. Ten six that might be good luck."

"Ok, Tony. I gotta go. Nice seeing you again," Angie said.

"Likewise, honey. Yawl take care. Young man, you take good care of my family. I can tell she cares deeply for you."

I didn't even give him a response. She pulled out into traffic and turned the volume up from her steering wheel, playing who else but The Diamond King.

Chapter 12

"Scarred by the boulevard
Bullied until I started giving bullies scars
Foreign broads in foreign cars
Hit me up for their pick me up
Murder bag in the stash box
Shoe box to place my knots
K's go CHOP CHOP CHOP
Out of the convertible, converting your top
Now bricks are the corner stones
Stone Ave. is where I get my corner on
Witness the making of a Diamond King
Etched in gold on my tombstone."

Angie said cheerfully, "I'm ready to turn
up. I slept well. My son was back home
sleeping in his room when I got there. I feel
blessed today."

"Ain't he staying with his father?" I
questioned.

"He is. He just came to get more clothes.
We talked for a while. He said his father is
doing a wonderful job listening and
understanding, because he had some of the
same experiences as a child. He's learning how
to be a man from a man. I never thought of it

that way. I'm going to give it a try and not allow myself to interfere with his father as much. We might not have been good for each other, but I know his intentions for our son is for him to be the best version of himself and not out here stealing and robbing."

"That's good to hear, Angie, seriously. Cause' brother's get a bad rap like we are all just dead beats, but there are mother's being dead beats using the system to separate the child from the father," I reminded her.

"We mother's carry our children for 9 months, so we build this bond that is just unexplainable. Feeling that life grow inside of us and moving around. The different sleep patterns they develop, morning sickness and just the experience of being one," she reminisced.

"I know yawl build a bond. But if a brother wants to be involved with his child, why is it such a competition instead of working together for the best interest of the child," I insisted.

"I can't speak for everybody else. For the most part, my son's father has been there without a doubt. He got behind in child support when he wasn't working. But other than that, he got himself back on track and never missed a payment since," Angie confessed.

"Child support? That shit is a joke. Some mother's use that to get back at fathers for whatever reason," I said, thinking about of few homies that were going through it.

"Yeah, I know a few, but it's always going to be some good with the bad."

Our social commentary was halted by Angie's horn as her hand came smashing down on it. Some lady stopped at the green light on her phone, instead of mashing the gas. "That texting and driving shit is out of hand," she said with an attitude.

"You be doing that shit too," I challenged her.

"Yeah, but I do it only at red lights. I try to be considerate. But if someone is calling with the tea, I will pull over on the side of the road to call. I gots to get the scoop, baby. That's what I do."

Angie added some extra lashes to her eyes. I don't normally like them, but I was just digging her vibe today. "What you looking at my feet for? I got my furry slides in the back just in case I got to come out of these heels. I was feeling jazzy today. That drive from the hospital really made me think about some things. A chaplin and two surgeons were talking to a lady informing her that her child didn't make it through surgery. Life is so temporary. I hugged my son without letting go once I saw him. I was thankful that he was alive and well."

"Yeah, that's the truth. When big momma passed away, I just never wanted to be in a hospital again. If it wasn't for how I feel for Ice, I would not have come. When it comes to funerals, people getting up lying be the same folk that didn't even visit at the hospital. That's why I don't stay the whole service," I painfully confessed.

"That's because you're different, Craft. You be on that otha' otha' shit. HAHAHA! You a comic book loving nigga with some decent dick," she said playfully.

"Shid. I done fucked with some comic book loving chicks that were straight freaks, so fuck what you talking about," I countered.

"That's all you like is freaks. All that money, no kids, no legacy just material stuff."

"Don't simmer me down to something as simple and plain as that. I like freaks. But shid, who don't like to be pleasured? I eat food for nourishment and pleasure, and I enjoy sex for nourishment and pleasure too," I informed her.

"How you get nourishment from sex? Cause' you like eating the box? Your head game is A++ by the way," she smiled.

"Girl, I'm serious! When that vibe is right, it's nourishment that I'm giving her and that she is giving me. Coming together communicating on our own frequency. Ain't nothing like it," I said confidently.

"What do you get, vitamins and minerals? Nigga, you say anything out your mouth," she said ignorantly.

"I get to peek into her soul. Sneaking behind her wall that she put up to keep me out. Penetrating her safe place. Exploring her world from the inside out."

"Where is the strangest place you ever had sex?" Angie interrupted.

"I don't know. It depends on what you call strange. I have had sex in a park in broad daylight before. The woods are very seductive…becoming one with nature."

"What yawl was doing? Hiking in the woods or something?" she said being nosey.

"Naw, we did it on a humble. We flipped a coin and went for it. She was facing the tree holding her skirt up with no panties. I was kissing on her neck, pleasuring her with my fingers. It was cool out. I think it was like the fall, cause' the leaves were beginning to turn orange and brown," I reflected.

"She must have been a freak; wearing a mini skirt with no panties on in the middle of winter," she said, hating.

"I said it was fall not winter."

Angie complained, "You said, you think it was fall. I don't want to hear about your little sexcapades anyway. That stuff ain't good for my Christian ears."

"Church girls have always been the funniest to have sex with. I fingered my girlfriend on the church van before," I relived.

"You ain't got no class. You will fuck anywhere."

"I was young. God didn't hold that against me."

"How old were you?" she asked.

"Old enough to keep an eye on the van driver while I wiggled my fingers under her zipper," I laughed.

"So, is that the "church girl" you talking about?"

"Naw, all I got was the finger. She ended up getting pregnant and marrying someone else. Sometimes, I still sniff this finger and think about her," I laughed, pointing my finger towards Angie's mouth like a magic wand. "Aw, shit girl, what you bite my finger for!"

"Cause' your little nasty ass finger should not have been in my face," she said pissed off.

Chapter 13

We pulled up in front of my old towering palace. My penthouse was burned to the ground and still smoldering. Nothing was salvageable. Sergeant Friendly was supposed to meet us here and give us a copy of the flash drive. Us meeting him here instead of revealing my hideout was the best move.

"We should have stopped and grabbed some breakfast. I'm hungry. All of these curves need to be fed," Angie said seriously.

I turned my eyes away from the rubble to look at her. "Yo ass always hungry. Put your hazard lights on, so we can peep the scene and be on the lookout for your homeboy." The hazard lights clicked at a rhythm that made me anxious for some reason. No good times replayed in my head no matter how hard I tried to reminisce. Nothing except how we fought our last time there. It's a great relief to start over, to begin again with better insight than my previous reign. Kids skipped school and had loud conversations about where they were meeting up at, cause' someone's mother was out of town. We did the same things, and we enjoyed it whether a punishment or a beating came after the skip party was over.

"Look at them fast ass lil girls knowing they need to be in school," Angie said as she blew her horn, and tried to get the skipping girl's attention.

"Get yawl asses in school!" she said like a foxy aunty.

They looked at Angie with a stare. "Mind your business lady. We living our best life," said the group of girls. They said their peace and went right back to texting, snap chattin,' and whatever else they were doing as they walked down the street.

"They know they need to be in school instead of being fast. That's how they get pregnant and be dropping out," Angie admitted.

"Girl, you skipped and chased boys too. Cut it out," I scolded.

"Bet if you had some daughters your happy ass tune would change."

"Yeah, you probably right, but I just remember being that age."

Angie changed the subject, "Let's check out that Diamond King video while we wait. I think you will enjoy the interview. He's discerning and intelligent for a man his age," she believed.

I interjected, "I ain't trying to hear nothing he talking about. Let that brother rest in paradise."

"It's funny you said something about paradise. He spoke on that in his interview. I'mma fast forward it towards the end where he speaks on paradise. I promise you will get a jewel out of it," she insisted.

I looked at my groupie ass partner with doubt. The contact should be here any minute, so it won't hurt to past time. "Go ahead, but if I don't like it, you owe me lunch, and this time, I'm picking the place."

"Deal, but I only treat to Big Barbs. I can't cheat on fam like that. If I'm spending it, I'm spending it with the fam," she said. Her finger glided across the screen of her phone to cue the video to the moment where he was discussing paradise. "This is the part I was telling you about. Checkout what he be saying."

My attention was out the window with my ears on the video.

The Diamond King:

".........Paradise is what you imagine it to be. Everyone doesn't aspire to have the golden roads and pearly gates theme of paradise."

Interviewer:

"What is paradise to you?"

The Diamond King:

"Being surrounded by those who love me, whether I have a penny to my name, or millions of dollars. Forward thinkers who can anticipate moves against me, insulating me from harm, because they believe in the totality of the vision."

Interviewer:

"How close are you to achieving paradise at this moment?"

The Diamond King:

"I'm achieving paradise by the second as we speak. Strengthening my spirit of discernment, and balancing the cravings of my flesh with the needs of my spirit."

Interviewer:
"Were there outside forces, or something internal that fostered this particular outlook?"

The Diamond King:
"My comfort zone caged me in, tarnished my outlook, and limited the way I perceived life. Now before you interrupt me with another question, allow me to elaborate further."

Interviewer:
"Please do!"

The Diamond King:
"I wanted more than just fame and money, a circle full of yes men that were just along for the ride, or women who were just hoping for a big pay day by having a baby by me. I've had a few mentors, but Charles "Fast Money" Manuel has helped me transition to see the world more holistically."

Interviewer:
"How so?"

The Diamond King:

"For one, by showing me the purpose of creating situations that feed my family and my associates' families for generations. For 2, everything in life is so temporary, so I don't get attached to the material things like I once did.

Interviewer:

"With a name like the Diamond King, it would seem that you are in love with the material world."

The Diamond King:

"I'm fortunate enough to recognize that I attract the finer things, but the finer things don't define me. I define me. Whether I'm in a shirt from the thrift store or rocking something custom.

Interviewer:

"I have a question from a fan through our IG account. Why did you and "B the Body" break up?"

The Diamond King:
"She chose to be concerned with issues that had nothing to do with my lack of loyalty. I love my fans, but yawl can't be so quick to believe everything you read on the internet."

Interviewer:
"Did you cheat on your girlfriend?"

The Diamond King:
"I have had sex with different women, but I never lost sight of her place in my life. She got the jewelry and the vacations. The dreams of weddings and a family. Giving me my first son, things I would only expect from my wife."

Interviewer:
"Don't you think that's kind of immature. To cheat in a relationship instead of being faithful or be single?"

The Diamond King:
"I just should have been honest in the beginning, giving her a choice to deal with this lifestyle. I'm still learning how to navigate through this lifestyle. I'm not ready to be tied

down by convention and what society deems to be a successful relationship."

Interviewer:
"How do you think your fans will receive your message of non-convention and essentially nonconformity?"

The Diamond King:
"My fans are open-minded. We live in a world much more different than that of our mother's and father's. We are evolving on a global scale.

The Diamond King (cont.):
Me and other entertainers have been put on a pedestal, and sometimes we fall short. Our shortcomings or areas in need of improvement are blasted all across the world before we have a chance to improve it, or admit to it being true."

Interviewer:
"Is it true that you once had sex on a million dollars cash?"

The Diamond King:
"No comment. Just know a million ain't enough for the Diamond King. The Making of a Diamond King is now available on all platforms."

Interviewer:
"Is that a yes or no?"

Chapter 14

I reached for the power button. "Turn this bullshit off," I said.

"What? He was finna turn up with a freestyle," she replied trying to get me to listen to more.

"It was enough of him for a while. Let that brother rest. He didn't even say nothing deep," I retorted.

"Maybe not to you, but his insight was well beyond the tender age of 25. He left way before his time," she explained.

"God don't make no mistakes, or he left before his time. Which is it church lady?" I taunted.

"It's a figure of speech. If you wasn't so busy fingering chicks on the back of the church van, then maybe you would be more compassionate," she combatted. "I go way back with him, so I'm speaking from a perspective that is personal and not from the eyes of a fan."

A rapid tap on the passenger side window got both of our attention. Two uniformed officers and neither one of them our contact. I began rolling down the window on the passenger side. Angie hesitated briefly before rolling down her driver's side window.

"May I help you officer?" rolled out her mouth in a cooperative tone.

"We have received several calls regarding a suspicious truck parked in front of the burned down building. I took the liberty of running your tags and I see you have a warrant out for your arrest," the officer announced.

"What I got a warrant for, officer? I don't do nothing, but work and go home," Angie said in disbelief.

"This is for an assault. Looks like you worked
someone over pretty bad."

"An assault! Who have I assaulted? They are lying, officer. I swear!"

Immediately the situation with Isis at the comedy club came to mind, but not out of my mouth. She started the shit and then wanted to press charges. I interrupted, "Excuse me officer…..."

The cop continued to stare at me. "Sir, let me see your I.D," he said, interrupting me in the process of defending my getaway driver. His breath smelled like stale coffee and shit candies. Spit gathered at the crack of his mouth as he continued to speak. I was familiar with the routine nodding while I reached for my wallet with one hand.

"Oh, you live here, huh? That was your place that burned down on the news? You look sneaky. It probably was some insurance shit. You rich niggas be too greedy," he said, turning his nose up at me.

The milder murder detective went to the car and ran my information. In the process, another squad car pulled up offering some assistance, I supposed. I nudged Angie with my elbow to get her attention. I turned to her briefly motioning with my head for her to look out the back. The cop on the driver side walked towards the other police car. If we were fugitives, we could have made a run for it.

"What's up with that extra police car? Your hands ain't lethal enough for that cat fight yawl had?" I mumbled. She motioned like a pugilist as I shadow boxed the air. Iron Angie Tyson in the flesh.

"Naw, seriously though, I'm scared kind of. My stomach is starting to feel nervousness and you know I talk too much when I'm nervous," she said, shaking.

"I ain't did shit! Who you gone snitch on, yourself?"

"I'm just saying, Craft, you bet not snitch on me. Snitches get stitches around these parts," she laughed throwing a few more punches of an offbeat three punch combination.

"Yo ass playing. I might not bail you out," I said, straightening up as last words came from my mouth.

"If you was that type of guy, I wouldn't be sitting here doing all of this with you. I know you got a sista's back," she insisted.

"It seems that you both have a meeting with our Sergeant. He told us that he is working on clearing up the confusion pertaining to these assault allegations. Sorry for the inconvenience folks. Have a good morning and enjoy the rest of your day," he said. He handed Angie both of our licenses. The cop with the white mess in the crack of his mouth chose to stay put in the squad car.

"Thank you, officer. You do the same," Angie said in a gracious and courteous way.

I paused for a moment. Zoned out staring at the still video of the Diamond King. I thought about how this arrogant muthafucka gonna brag about stealing my money and fucking my broad. If he wasn't already dead, I would kill his ass.

"I'm glad that went that way, cause' I'm looking way to cute to be wearing a jumpsuit, boo. You best believe that." She looked in the rearview mirror while touching up her lip gloss. The Sergeant exited his car and made his way towards us.

"About time that nigga defended me with action instead of being a good guy. A good guy is fine, but I like to know my man can whoop a nigga ass, if need be. Hell, at least try. Like you do Craft……Craft!"

I could hear her clearly, but I wasn't able to move. I was stuck looking at his image wishing I was the one that sent him and his smirk to the afterlife.

"Yeah, you right. You gotta' be balanced in life. Sometimes you got to be red handed with gloves on," I said without even thinking to keep up the cadence of the conversation.

"What does that even mean? You need to make you a calendar of meaningless quotes. I bet you know 366 plus," Angie exaggerated.

The Sergeant walked to the driver's side of the truck. His lights flashed, so everything seemed official. "I see you guys have had an eventful morning so far," he smiled showing off his new dental work.

He was freshly shaven. My face was in need of some pampering from Ice. I was out here looking like I needed a bath and a dollar. I pulled down the mirror in front of me and analyzed my face. The shadow around my beard was thicker than usual. Bags were under my eyes from stress. I was carrying a heavy load. I closed the mirror and reminded myself that I was in grind mode.

"Mr. Craft, you are looking fine, sir, for all that you have been through. Keep your head up," said Officer Sassy trying to cheer me up. He passed Angie a small yellow envelope that had to be the video of the person who possibly burned down my palace in the sky.

"You probably will be questioned once again to at least to see if you can I.D. the person on this video. I'm giving you a heads up," he warned.

"I appreciate it. I will definitely take a look at this video to see if I can be of any help in finding the perpetrators that murdered my friend and tried to destroy my life." I mimicked a victim eagerly ready to cooperate like on one of them many cop shows. I was not cooperating at all. Just fact finding to wrap this shit up myself.

"Angie, again I am sorry for the other day. It was just the best hand to play. I wasn't in anyway going to allow you to be harmed," he said, placing his hand on her forearm revealing his wedding band. She immediately removed her arm from the clutch of his grasp.

"That's fine. I know what it is like to have to keep your job. We all got bills," Angie said disgusted. Angie was lying. Most of the dudes she liked were knuckle draggers. He wished us well and walked back to his car.

"He used to try and talk to me. He had the nerve to wear his wedding ring. Yawl niggas ain't shit," she said disappointingly.

"I'm not finna be the spokesperson for niggas everywhere. Drive me to my spot that is still standing, so we can watch this video and I can get cleaned up."

"You need to shave. Your face look like it stank."

I ignored her petty insult. Instead, I maneuvered and came back with one of my own. "How long you and o'l boy been fucking around?" I said, poking the beehive.

Her eyes began to widen. Her face turned ugly. I knew I won a petty prize. "For your information, we ain't never fucked or did anything else. I'm glad I didn't either. I want a nigga that will lose a job defending me," she said, beginning to raise her voice.

"You just told the man job well done. Now you telling me something different."

"I told him what was necessary to remain valuable to us, and us valuable to him. It wasn't about telling him the truth. You of all people should know that," she poked back.

"I'm just saying, free my nigga, Angie until my nigga Angie free," I instigated pissing her off even more.

"Boy, don't play like that. While you was zoned out, he said he knows Isis. He will speak to her on my behalf to get this mis-understanding situated. He said something about his wife knowing her momma or something. I just hope he get it taken care of," she worried.

She reached to restart the video. I stopped her before she got a chance to restart it. She responded, "I don't know what type of problem yawl had that got you disliking a dead man this much. But I'm a fan, so let me listen to one of my favorite entertainers." I acquiesced and looked down at my phone to check the incoming message for some good news.

11:17 a.m.
Isis: I will drop the charges if you do that thing for me.
(I left the text on read and didn't reply. I'd rather listen to the Diamond King.)

"Don't be texting none of your hoes. We out here solving crimes against humanity and shit. They gotta wait until we save the day!" Angie shouted on cue.

"Why your ass always gotta be so extra?" I asked, Ms. Thickums.

"Why my extra always gotta be too much?" she replied. Neither question was answered. Another stalemate in our long history of conversations. She pressed play and my ex-stepson began talking like an asshole much older than he really is.

"Listen to how mature he sounds," Angie admired getting her preferred fix of fandom. I drifted off into a place where peace used to be my refuge. Over time, I've learned to find solace in war as well. I was eager to see who plucked me from the heavens like Lucifer. The rain came down gently from multiple angles splashing down on the windows of her truck. It used to be immaculate on the inside. Now it looked more lived in. Our stake outs have been eventful, but I haven't gotten the clarity that I have hoped for. I may be lullabied to sleep and fed to the wolves by my driver. She hasn't been anything, but helpful so far. Unc and Ice don't feel she belongs with us, but I see her extrinsic value that they don't see. It's the things that they might see that I don't that got me pretending to have my eyes closed completely.

"Hey, wake up. You can't be sleep that fast. Listen to this part," Angie urged eagerly. In fact, she was a little too eager for me to listen to that dude. Many of the things he said sounded like me for a reason. I'm the original, but I guess the shiny replicas float her boat better."

I reminded Angie, "I don't want to listen to him anymore. I'm meditating on the necessary moves to make. I got pieces to move from the board still."

"I hope you don't think you're moving me. I've put in too much work to not be considered valuable," she replied.

"You sound more entitled than valuable right now," I revealed.

"I am entitled. I don't just put my neck out for anybody," Angie admitted with emphasis.

"I'm not suggesting you do, but I do expect you to play your part. That is essential to any team moving forward," I instructed.

"Haven't I played my part?" she asked.

"I'm honestly still trying to figure out what part are you playing, and what position I need you to play."

"What you mean? What position you need me to play?" she came back quickly.

"Look, I'm the quarterback, the coach, team owner and…..."

Angie interrupted, "Damn! Well…..."

"Don't be cutting me off!" I demanded.

"Excuse me for breathing."

"Can you be a receiver if I need you to be?" I asked.

"Yeah, I guess so, but when would you need me to catch the ball?" she inquired.

"Sometimes, I need you to listen and block for me. Maybe even run a play by keeping the ball. Can you do that for me?" I asked keeping the metaphor going.

"Me and my BD used to run up and down the interstate way back when before he got caught up. So, I'm used to making plays and making moves," she responded.

"I can see that part clearly. You got a lot of hustle about yourself. Sometimes you get nervous and make the wrong moves by speaking when listening is key," I reminded her.

She admitted, "Yeah, I definitely need to work on that. But other than that, I'm good for the team."

"The good isn't the question. It's the longevity. Legacy establishing and legacy protecting good. My business is meant for generations after us. This isn't a fly by night, or flash in the skillet type of situation," I said.

"I understand," she agreed.

"We will see how much you understand later," I mumbled.

"I don't want to…..."

Before she could finish, I said, "Stop right there. It's not what you want that is important. It is what is needed for me and the business.

That is the priority and should be your priority."

"The business?" she fired back with an attitude.

"The business…This blood in, blood out… ain't no retirement lunches."

"Nigga, that sound like some cult shit to me," she protested.

"Pull over right here," I demanded.

"I can't. It's a car right……"

"PULL OVER NOW GODDAMMIT!" I yelled at the top of my lungs.

She pulled over to the edge of the street. She damn near side swiped a car and I didn't give a shit. I reached in my jacket pocket unsheathing my 9. It was already cocked and safety free. Her eyes got big. She began to get nervous.

"What's the gun for? Do you need me to grab mines?" she said, attempting to reach for her pistol in her stash box.

"Naw. Two guns is one too many. What are you here for?" I asked while gritting my teeth as I turned to look at her.

"Cause' you asked me too."

"Is that the only reason? I said.

"No, I mean I like being around you. We have fun, but you know I always like being around you," she insisted.

"We ain't on no hanging out shit right now. This shit we on is murder, if necessary. That pink pistol ain't seen no action. This gun has bodies. The blood of enemies, friends, and family alike has had the displeasure of being on the receiving end of God's Promise," I said coldly.

"You named your gun God's Promise?"

"Everything I said and you're more intrigued with the name?" I continued as she shrugged her shoulders like Kanye.

Breaking it down, I revealed, "It was the name necessary for it. It helps me keep God's Promise in the physical realm while God's keeps His in the spiritual realm."

"What is God's Promise?" she inquired further.

"That's an answer for another time. But this answer can't wait," I said, pausing for a moment.

"Which is what?"

"How long have you been a cop?" I asked.

"A cop? Who me? Boy, I ain't working for the boyz. You got me fucked up with that!" she insisted.

I frisked her to see if she was wearing a wire. If she was, I would personally remove her from the board right then. Today was D Day. Actions must be taken. Positions and intentions needed to be solidified. The words rambled through my head at a fast, blurring pace.

"This shit ain't funny. Get off of me!" she cursed.

I grabbed the phone that had me so paranoid. The camera looked as if it was looking at me and recording us.

"Are you recording us? Answer me now, goddammit! I ain't have you pullover without reason," I raged.

"You're scaring me, Craft. Chill out…...," Angie said, trembling.

"Answer me!" I demanded.

"No Craft. I ain't wearing no wire. If that gunplay shit was trying to get me in the mood, it didn't work," she replied annoyed.

"You better not be no fucking cop or working against me. I will end you my muthafuckin self!" I promised.

"What type of shit is that? I mean, damn. I do all of this. I even go see your one chick with you in the hospital. I beat up a chick that was on some other shit. I drove you to go see Big I. I don't know if you need a joint or some pussy, but call me when you cool," she ranted. She opened her door and got out into traffic before remembering that she was the owner.

Angie exploded, "This my shit! You gotta find your own way to your spot. I ain't gonna be dealing with this type of mistrust pulling out rusty guns like you the only nigga that caught bodies."

I smirked at her venting and placed the gun back into my inside pocket.

"That shit ain't funny. You got to go, Craft. That was too far!"

"Girl, I ain't' going nowhere. Let's go, so we can get this business handled," I said impatiently. Her clothes were slightly wet from the drizzling rain. She sat speechless and gripped the steering wheel with both hands. The truck didn't move when she pressed down on the gas.

"The truck is in neutral. We ain't going nowhere like that Angie."

She shifted the truck into park and began to cry as she hit me on my shoulder. I grabbed her arm like I would do Stormy when she was having her fits. I should have kissed her. I should have reassured her like I would have in a time before. But holding her arms allowed her to release her tension. There were no hazard lights this time to tick and blink me into numbness. It was just beeping horns as they drove by peering into the truck in the process.

"My dad did that to my mom before. I don't play with guns. That shit is serious. We don't point guns at people we love, or at least care about. You are a cold-hearted bastard," she sobbed.

No words or rebuttal to her flow, I just let her release to see what she would say and how she would react.

"He was drunk one day……," she started. Her storytelling was broken up by the tears as mascara raced down her face. "He was drunk and pulled a gun out on her. He threatened to kill her because he thought she was cheating on him. No proof, no nothing, just a gut feeling he would say. I can still hear the hammer being cocked back. I can smell the cabbage and corned beef, his favorite, burning on the stove," she replayed from her memories. She shifted the truck into drive. She damn near wrecked into a car on her driver's side before retaking control of her emotions.

"How many people have you told that story to?" I probed.

"Why nigga? If I told anyone besides you, I ain't loyal or something? Worthy or some shit. What is it now?" Angie wondered.

"Tell me something you never told anyone. Something you never told any other man, or that no more than a handful of people know about you."

"I ain't on your bi-polar ass games. I'm ready to drop you off and get on with my day. I could be doing something else besides slaving for you!"

"Oh, so now you're slaving? At first, it was where you wanted to be. You see how stories change up just that quick," I said, trying to catch her in a lie.

"Fuck you! You changed up on me and pulled a gun out on me," she spoke angrily.

"Yeah, I did and fuck you too! I got to protect my muthafuckan family. I told you it is family and friends on the receiving end of this promise and all of them deserved it."

"You're crazy," she insisted.

"I'm crazy, because I want to know the truth. You're crazy for not wanting to know the truth," I mocked.

"What truth? My BD use to shoot niggas all the time. I'm not impressed by guns and shit like that. Of course, I've seen some things on the road that I won't repeat or share with you or anyone else. I gravitate to you, because you bring a different energy. I ain't familiar with this paranoid nigga," Angie replied dismissing me.

Chapter 15

We were a block or so from my place. I needed a shower before even looking at the video. If my arms smelled like ass, I could only imagine what my ass smelled like. "I ain't paranoid. I'm unconventional maybe. At the end of the day, ain't no apology coming from me to you. It was necessary to see if you would break. I need to know how you will respond under pressure," I noted heartlessly.

"You seem to be the one not responding well due to the circumstances which I know is a lot," she said, softening for a moment.

"I'm making sure that you belong on the board. That you are willing to do whatever is necessary. We are coming to the end of the game."

"My life ain't a game," she pointed out.

"Maybe not to you, but in life, we are all pawns on someone else's chess board," I said.

"On my chessboard I'm the......"

I stopped her, "You're the what? Go ahead and say it."

"Well, I damn sure ain't no pawn on my chessboard, so I ain't gonna be one on yours," she assured.

"I don't want you too. Sometimes. how you start out ain't how you finish."

"That's your opinion. Maybe I don't want to play chess. Maybe I gotta hand as in spades. I'm running it like I'm trying to get 10 books," she admitted.

"Cool, who is your partner?" I said, playing along.

"I'm my partner if I have to be. My point is I'mma play the hell out of what I have to, to get what I need to get. Me and my son ain't never went without. We damn sure ain't finna start now," she explained.

"Get out of your feelings. It ain't about that. I'm glad your son will be with his father learning the ropes."

"Is that because you think I'mma be something you can use up and throw away....I ain't going for that shit. Our friendship, relationship, partnership doesn't have to have titles. It ain't necessary," she concluded.

We pulled up to my loth with my title-less companion. The rain smelled like the first day of school. The fresh air was conveniently replaced by the stench of grey paint layered thickly upon the walls. It masked the graffiti and obscenities that covered up the expressions of many years past. Angie looked like she wanted to explode with anger. She was like a cute little caramel colored poodle ready to snap. Repair men painted the utility poles and clogged traffic with their white trucks and orange cones and disabled a whole lane unnecessarily. Any guy with a hard hat doing construction or installing cable was possibly working for the law. That was what was passed down to me from my older cousins and movies we grew up watching. Yet several decades later, those words permeated my mind, and I always double the block just in case.

"Angie. Girl, straighten up your face. I know you ain't still mad at me?" She never even looked in my direction. Keeping her eyes focused on the road, she doubled the block as if to say I already know what to do. Her eyes showed the same pent-up rage that I've seen many times before. Silently counting to 10, preventing yourself from doing something you might later regret. The tires screeched as she came to an abrupt halt at the stop sign. My body jerked forward. My arm extended out automatically as if preventing myself from going through the windshield.

"What the fuck you smash on the breaks that hard for! It ain't shit in front of us," I yelled.

She turned her head slightly just enough to see a part of the right side of her face and I said, "Your ass looking at me crazy like you wearing a neck brace. What the hell is your problem?"

"My bad. I saw the sign late. You good. It ain't like we hit something or nothing." I ignored her. She wanted attention. But I was going to defunk and change clothes, watch the video, and see who this fire bug was that torched my house.

"I'm just going to drop you off. I'm not going up with you. I'm not in the mood. I'm going to go and see if my son needs help packing up his stuff or something," she detailed.

"I ain't hearing none of that. We got business to handle. He is becoming a man. I'm sure he doesn't need you to match up his outfits and shit like that," I said annoyed.

"You don't know what he needs."

"I know what you need and it's to get your ass up them stairs and let's finish up this business. We can discuss your concerns in further detail after I freshen up. We are very close to resolving this issue. It will in turn solve issues for people that I hold dear to me and their families, yours included even if you decide in this moment that you don't want to join me for the next chapter."

She gazed at me. She was ready to tear up again, because she knew I was telling the truth, and that no matter what I fucks with her the long way. "You be acting like you the only one with shit going on. That shit with my son is so hard for me right now. This has helped me. It keeps my mind off things, sort of, but I can't help but wonder if I'm trading one hell for another one."

"Angie, in life you either selling heaven to the people or crowns to kings. If you ain't doing the selling, 9 times out of 10 you're doing the buying. I'm not promising you paradise and a life without stress or worries, failures, or hard times. I'm letting you know that you won't be in that season forever, nor will you go through things alone. This is family first then business, but you must understand wholeheartedly that my family is my business," I reminded her.

"You be acting like I'm slow. I get all of that. You always were the one that was more serious out of everybody. I guess I'm more concerned with everything else. I know you ain't no angel or no devil either. You are somewhere in the middle where you embody the qualities or lack of qualities of both an angel and devil."

Hahaha. "That just sounds human to me. That sounds like everyone I know. Why the hell you got to get all religious with it?" I wondered.

"You know what I'm saying. You really can make hell or heaven on earth for a person. Even though you didn't kill Big I yourself, you watched him being murdered," she said truthfully.

"That shit was justice! Murder is when someone is innocent. Naw, I don't agree with the murder cops' tactics, but dammit the rage I felt, damn right, I watched his execution. I have literally given that man money for his family, cause' I felt he would do the same for me and never ask for it back. His knife to my back was different, cause' I fucked with him

101

like a muthafuckan brother. I know you ain't choosing sides?" I asked.

"I ain't choosing sides with that comment. I chose sides by being with you that first moment, and I never left your side. I ain't no young girl thirsty for excitement and adventure. I'm motivated by long term plans too. Yeah, I want a hero. Shit what woman don't want a superman if she can have one. I don't want to do everything by myself just to show that I'm a strong woman. Fuck every bit of that. I want my life to be more meaningful and I'm defining it right this moment. I ain't waiting on no nigga to save me like I'mma a damsel in distress tied to the train track. Sometimes, I'm the conductor driving the train about to run me a muthafucka over."

Chapter 16

Thunder chiseled the sky. Rain pelted everything like the force of hail. Romantic and haunting, the sky went from a greyish hue to something dark with hints of a red glow in the shadows like the reaper was creeping up from behind.

"I got a taste for some barbecue," Angie switched modes out of the blue.

"Girl, Big Barbs don't sell barbecue today. That's on Friday's and Saturday's. I know you trippin' as much as you eat there," I said half annoyed.

"Boy, I know my spots. It's this new place up the road I want to check out."

"Well, come on up and order the food. They can deliver it to us. This weather is nasty, and we got to get moving," I advised.

"You finna' shower anyway. I know you didn't think I was giving your moody disrespectful ass none of this when we got upstairs. Hop in the shower and I will be back by the time you get out. At least have a towel on," she said, looking me up and down.

"Go get the food and bring your ass back here. I'll be chillin' in the tub. You can join me when you get back," I replied pulling a few green strips from my pocket and putting them in her hand. When I kissed her forehead, she gave me that cute you get on my nerves look. The scented herbal oil on her short wavy hair flowed up my nose like smoke from a blunt of Cali. I wiped the tears from her eyes, smearing the mascara even more. "Wipe your face before you go into that restaurant. You're looking like an evil clown," I joked.

She laughed while looking into the vanity mirror in her truck. "Don't worry about me. I got some stuff in my purse. I won't embarrass myself like that."

I placed a spare key in her hand before heading upstairs. Me and Ice have hustled on and celebrated many holidays here. Before things became unfamiliar. Before we became more familiar with each other. We regretted nothing and didn't accept anything on face value. The air in the hallway had an aroma: instant nostalgia like somebody been in there cooking oxtails stew. Stormy used to make it for me with rice, peas, and steamed cabbage. That shit used to be bangin'. A crockpot full of oxtails were slowly simmering in some thick gravy. Sprigs of fresh rosemary and thyme were on the counter with garlic bulbs and shallots.

Dried seasonings were neatly placed in the corner by the microwave. I moved from room to room and couldn't find anyone. No clothes, no sign of a break-in, nothing. Only person it could be was Stormy, but I got the keys from her crazy ass the last time we spoke. No answer. Her phone kept going to voicemail. I ain't finna' shower or shit til' I find out who chef'n in my house. But on some weird shit, I can't wait till the food get done. They look good then a muthafucka.

I grabbed some buds from my cigar box in my humidor. Exotic citrus flavor I copped from my weed guy. "Fuck it. I need to smoke me one to gather my thoughts and see what the fuck is going on," I said, marching back and forth from the closet to the living room. I grabbed clothes to wear and constantly looked out of the window. The rain was still coming down, but not one car was out of place. Who breaks into your shit, cooks something and leaves and not call, text, write a note, or something? Let me call Angie. She should've been back by now. Whoever the fuck been in here cooking should have been back. They are trying to burn my shit down. I turned the bath water off, only to hear a key turning to unlock the door.

"Angie about time you got here. I was just finna' call you." To my surprise, it wasn't Angie. It was the mystery chef with a plastic grocery bag in her hand. "Stormy what the fuck you doing here? How the fuck you get a key to my house!"

"Well damn, I miss you too. I tried to do something nice, and this is the thanks I get," she pouted, but her eyes in puppy dog mode ain't working today.

"What are you doing here?" I demanded puffing the blunt while I walked back over to the crockpot.

"They should be done shortly. I knew you would love my surprise." BAM! I slammed the lid on the crockpot. "You know I don't like fucking surprises unless I'm the one doin' the surprising." I grabbed the crockpot and tossed it out of the kitchen window. "Get your funky ass out of my house and I ain't calling no police."

"Why the hell you throw the damn food out of the window?"

I snatched the cord out of the socket and folded it like a belt. The door opened, forcing me to pause and direct my attention elsewhere. Finally, Angie was back with the food.

"Well, hell if I knew you had company, I would have brought more food," Stormy said in delusion. Angie and Stormy began sizing each other up, nodding heads as Angie walked to the dining area, placing the bags on the table.

"Well damn. Don't everybody speak at once," Angie said, walking towards me. "Hey, I'm Angie. We've met before. I don't know if you remember me."

"Yeah, I remember you. Um.. hi," Stormy replied as dry as the barbecue that Angie disrespected my house with.

"This meat kinda' dry, Angie," I complained as I dipped it in the barbecue sauce. Feeling kinda buzzed, I began walking towards Stormy for answers.

"I ain't come over here to start shit, Craft. I came over here, because I know where Shona Evans might be laying low at," Stormy explained.

Furious, I replied, "Well, bitch you should have brought her to me not her whereabouts! I don't trust your rotten ass anyway. We were better than that little bullshit you pulled wit' the young nigga."

"This is not about that," she insisted.

"You don't come to my house dictating what anything is about. You violated!" I said as I took a deep puff, held the smoke in, then blew it in Stormy's direction.

She began to speak, "I violated, nigga……"

Cutting her off in mid-sentence, I continued, "Nigga what? I am what I have always been. You know that! Don't gimme no excuses to why you would fuck a nigga I raised."

"Damn, Craft. I didn't know your shit was so messy from the outside looking in it," Angie said sarcastically.

"Shut up Angie!" she continued to gnaw on the dry smokey barbecue with the whateva' nigga look on her face.

I demanded, "Where is she, Stormy? Fuck it! That's the big picture anyway."

"She's been hiding in a battered women's shelter that the church owns," Stormy revealed.

"Did Bishop know about this shit? Better yet, who told your ass her top-secret location?" I questioned her suspiciously.

"I know a few people who work in that field, and I was going to lunch with a friend when I saw her. She looked like she was beaten up pretty bad. I thought you caught up with her already," Stormy claimed.

"Naw, she on borrowed time right now. We ain't found her yet, but she definitely will be punished. You didn't come over here and cook just to tell me that. You could have called or texted me this information," I told her.

"I changed my number. Knowing that you've tried to call me at least once since our big fallout means a lot to me. Awww, you missed me baby?" she taunted.

"Bitch, the only reason you still living now is, because I missed you."

"Craft your food is getting cold. Can I get your fries? You know cold fries are not good at all," Angie asked.

I motioned with my hand yeah and shut up at the same time as my mother used to do to us when her soaps were on. "You got plenty of big nuts showing your face in my place and give me my key. How did you get another one?" I probed.

"I been had this key. You know I'm bad with keys. I keep multiple copies." She handed me the Snoopy key that had a slight bend to it like all her other keys.

"Why you always….never mind," I paused quickly stopping myself from continuing.

"I don't mean to break up yawl pow wow, but we got shit to do today. Craft your funky ass need to hit that water. I hope you washed your hands before you dug in that food," Angie intervened.

"Girl, don't be barking no orders. My bath water ready. I'm on my way in, but I got an intruder alert before I had a chance to get this old flavor off."

"Is she staying or going?" Angie the field general kept barking orders as Stormy began walking into the bathroom disrobing as she went.

"What the fuck you doing, girl? You ain't finna dirty up the water." Her turquoise thong was the last piece that she threw off onto the trail of clothes in the hallway. She was welcomed by the water as she sat in.

"Thanks for running my bath water. I used to have to beg you to clean out the tub. I guess this time away has done us both some good. Angie would you be so kind to give us some privacy while we bathe please," Stormy said while motioning her hand like a queen to a peasant.

"You ain't gotta go nowhere, Angie. Stormy getcho' messy ass out of that tub and out of my house!" I demanded.

"Come make me!" she dared.

Chapter 17

Before I could head towards the bathroom, Angie beat me to it. "Angie come back here! Girl, don't go in there," I stated then grabbed her arms and attempted to calm her down. Stormy splashed water and screamed at the top of her lungs.

"She on some super disrespectful shit. See I be trying to turn over a new leaf, but people always testing my gangsta," Angie reminded me.

"Everything is good…...." I assured her. CRACK! Stormy swung hitting me in the back of the head. Angie started swinging at Stormy. Mayhem is everywhere I go lately. Pictures started falling from the wall in the hallway. I snatched Stormy shit starting ass up and tossed her on the bed. Angie trailed me swinging. She was hitting me in the back of the head.

"Angie chill the fuck out with all of that wild shit!" I said unfazed by her punches.

"She started it," Angie replied in a familiar way. Stormy's naked, wet body was agile and well-shaped. It flung around like a weapon on the bed.

"Stop now! Stormy chill your ass out!" I yelled flashing back to the times that I no longer wanted to repeat. To times I'm glad are over. Angie rushed me and threw me off balance. I fell into the barbell rack. She jumped on the bed to fight Stormy.

"SHIT!" I hit my baby toe on the base of the black rack that barely budged when I crashed into it. Stormy kicked her directly in the midsection. Angie flew into the T.V. mounted on the wall, causing the mount to bend and the screen to crack. I knew then there would be no breaking up that fight. Like momma use to say, somebody ass is paying for this. Angie grabbed her back in agony while rushing back into the fray. She outweighed Stormy by 50 lbs, but Stormy was a fighter at heart. Also, I thought apparently she like fucking young niggas too.

"Bitch, I'm gone fuck you up!" Angie boasted, landing a hard punch to the side of Stormy's head. The punch was so hard the birds flew from the trees outside. Angie began to choke Stormy once she realized she was dazed. The harder Angie choked her the harder Stormy bit her arm causing blood to gush from the wound. This shit was embarrassing, but

Stormy came over uninvited and got that medicine she needed to calm her ass down some. Stormy kicked wildly connecting directly into Angie's chest forcing her off the bed. The shear force caused them to fall on the floor, rolling around punching and biting. Exhausted, breathing heavy they both paused momentarily. Angie's nice outfit was torn exposing her augmented breast, plump and artificial, but oh so juicy.

"Bitch, you thought I was dressed too cute to hand out ass whoopins? My sto' open 24/7,"Angie barked jumping back to her feet ready for another round.

Stormy without warning hopped to her feet and threw a punch, but I caught her fist in the air. "Enough of this. I'm tired of your trouble making ass. Get the fuck out of my house!"

"You want me to leave? You choosing her over me? We got history. Your future can't happen without me," Stormy said in disbelief.

"Get the fuck out of here! I was good before you and I will be good after you."

"You don't want me to leave now. Since the fighting is out of the way we can get down to business," she backtracked.

"Bitch, is you crazy? You come up here on your Martha Stewart, Mike Tyson shit and you acting like I'm supposed to bow down to your uninvited ass."

The Fatal Attraction said, "I'm never letting you free, Craft. I will swallow the key and jump off of a bridge first."

"You hilarious. I don't need freeing. If I did, I wouldn't need you to free me."

"Bitch, you want to go again," Angie huffed while catching her breath."

"Pipe that shit all the way down. I ain't scared of a fight. Craft know I ain't no lightweight. I'm a pretty yella' bitch who ain't scared to hit," Stormy informed Angie.

"This silly bitch. Reciting song lyrics don't make you gangsta. Let's go! I'm still here ready to hit?" Angie said.

Stormy came back quickly, "Bitch having yawl hoes writing songs about me makes me gangsta."

"Hoe, you must have hit your head. Diamond King ain't write that about you," Angie laughed.

"Ask itchy dick over there," Stormy barked pointing in my direction.

"My dick ain't itchy. I don't know if he did or not write the song for her, but she sucked his dick for sure though."

"Nigga, you throwing shade don't dim the light on these facts and you know that," she gathered herself while Angie began locating her clothes.

I tossed her messy ass out like those oxtails. "You lucky I ain't toss your ass down them steps," I said.

"Wait! Wait ok. Craft, I know the other stuff too. I know where Tags is hiding too," she grinned like a Chester cat as if to say I told you I wasn't going anywhere.

"Whatchu grinning for? Go clean that shit off of the sidewalk and bring your tattle telling ass back up here," I demanded. She grabbed the broom and a garbage bag wearing nothing but a T-shirt.

"Get your phone and put it on the counter," I instructed her.

"What you need my phone for?" she asked. The look I gave her was enough to answer her curiosity. She pranced back in this time wearing panties with her T shirt, and slammed the phone down on the countertop near Angie's food trying to get a reaction. Angie,

116

unbothered never looked up. She was flipping the bones and soggy white bread back and forth playing with her food.

"Get that other phone your ass ain't slick," I requested.

"Oh, baby. I forgot about that phone. You know that's my business phone."

I could always tell when she was lying, and it aggravated me sometimes.
"Yeah, I bet you did. Just put all your damn clothes on. You ain't got to be seen. That lil side show you had poppin' is all over wit," I ridiculed.

She mumbled something under her breath like the spoiled rotten entitled brat that she was. I didn't even feed into it. I was looking at the new mess that she came and made.

"Angie, you ok baby? You awfully quiet."

"I'm quiet, because I know how I can get. I gave her a fair one on the strength of you. I know you still love her. I can tell how you look at her. Even your hate carries love's spirit for her," she revealed.

"I love her, but this isn't about love. It's about resolving this issue. We discussed this already."

Stormy did too much for me to embrace her back into my life. A different version of me would have put that bitch's face on a milk carton and her body somewhere never to be found. I thought to myself as Angie continued talking about whatever she was talking about. My house was reflecting my life: cluttered, broken, with a stench that I couldn't seem to wash off. I stood in silence disgusted with myself. My high blown, I was seething with anger. I observed the gravity of the situation like a fly on the wall.

"Angie, let's get in the tub and get cleaned up," I invited her holding out my hand. She acquiesced, placing her hand into mines and followed me to the bathroom. We didn't say much of anything, just walked to the back, stepping over the train wreck that Stormy caused. I made my way to the tub adjusting the temperature and jet settings while my partner in crime headed towards the shower. I didn't question her. I knew she wanted to have some time alone.

"You can tell you fuck plenty of bitches all these good smelling body washes and lotions. I might have to steal this shampoo and conditioner," she stared, undressing like she had been on her feet all day.

"Just take a shower and use whatever you need and how much you need too. Yo ass always gotta be extra."

I sat there soaking and watching her shower. The water ran like rain crashing down rolling off her beautiful titties. The rag was sudsy as she washed and scrubbed herself, removing all that was unappealing and stressful from the day. I wanted to respect her space, but I want to invade her space just a little bit too.

"I see you looking at me. This is a huge bathroom. I need one of these automatic steam showers for my place," Angie said, interrupting my thoughts as I was trying to talk myself out of showering with her.

"You know you wanted me to shower with you," I said, reversing the conversation.

"We both know that if we wanted it, it would happen rather it's the shower, the tub or anywhere else for that matter." The honesty and certainty of her words was causing my semi erection to swell under the water as she began teasing me with the sway of her tongue.

"I hope I didn't interrupt anything. Who should I join?" the buzz killing bitch said as she returned. "I think I'm in the mood to take a warm bath. I almost cut myself, but one of those nice workers came over and helped me," she bragged. Stormy gestured trying to get into the tub with me.

" Ain't no reigniting that flame. I am disgusted by the sight of you." I said.

"I need to get this gravy off me. You know I like my gravy in me. I miss drinking yours," she taunted.

I snatched her with my proud erection looking not so proud now swinging at my thigh.

"What's the matter you cold or something, Craft? Stormy teased.

I pushed her out of the way making my way over to Angie. Stormy being Stormy watched us as she submerged her scratched and bruised body into the slightly murky water just like a crocodile waiting to attack. I stood behind Angie. She turned to me and began to wash my body with her soapy rag.

"I guess it worked out for us anyway, babe," I smiled.

"I guess it did, Craft. I'm glad you got in here with me. I wish we had more time to be alone and enjoy our moments differently. O'l girl in that dirty ass water with her messy ass," Angie said, glancing over at Stormy.

I placed my finger on her lips and began kissing her neck. Just like clockwork, Stormy heaved the remote control into the shower area. It crashed against the green goldstones I placed in the shower for healing properties. Stormy's eyes became large, red and enraged as she charged the massive open shower. Everything unraveled in slow motion like the universe was timing things perfectly. Crack! Bang! A straight shot to the chin left Stormy and her messy ass attitude unconscious on the floor.

"I told that bitch to quit fucking with me. I got hands for real. Play play that lil' weak bitch!" Angie shouted ready for the next round.

The mood passed us both. My dick was unconscious. I was tired. Finally washed up, I stepped over the twice defeated opponent who begged for a title match. Angie dried off and tossed the towel on top of Stormy covering her face completely.

"She tore up my fuckin' clothes. I need something to wear," she said.

"Grab a T-shirt and a pair of my sweats."

"I'mma just grab a pair of your basketball shorts. Is anything off limits?"

"Get whichever ones you want on' care." I headed to the living room wearing just my towel still dripping water.

"Wishing I wouldn't have tossed that stew out. I'm hungry then a muthafucka right about now!" I said disappointed.

Angie came into the living room wearing a white dress shirt and my basketball shorts. "This shirt just screamed at me, so I said, ok." She laughed for the first time in what seemed like forever. I wasn't trippin' off no shirt, plus she looked sexy in it.

"Order us something to eat while I look for the video that we need to watch. All this damn chaos, I fucked around and misplaced it." I searched endlessly for the damn flash drive.

"What do you want me to order?" Angie questioned.

"Shid, some oxtails from the Caribbean spot. A number 17 with extra oxtails and gravy on my yellow rice. Tell them it's an order for Craft and to please put a rush on it."

"Oh, so you the king of the tails huh," she said sarcastically. I noticed the admiration in her voice.

"I'mma be crowning that tail later on," I admitted returning my mind to the gutter.

"I can't wait either. After a day like this, I want to relax and unwind. I feel tense and knotted up. See look, feel right here with those strong hands of yours."

I gripped her shoulders firmly. She started looking at me like she was fucking me with her eyes again. I couldn't even get back in the zone. Right now, it was business first. I abruptly stopped and began to look for Stormy's car keys.

"Why you stop? It started to feel good. You a tease bae."

"This good dick keep me in enough trouble as it is. Have you seen Stormy's keys? I wonder did her ass pick them up accidentally on purpose," I said, looking around.

"Check her pants or her purse," Angie directed while covering the phone placing the order. Hey, they said ok. They will be here right away. You must order from there or tip big, cause' they was on it on it."

"I treat people accordingly how they treat me most of the time, so best believe they reciprocate the love."

"Here go her keys!" Angie dangled them.

"She got more keys than a maintenance man," I noticed as they jingled. I instantly recognized that she had another key to this place and my other place.

"Who the fuck keep making her all of these keys!" was the first thought that surged from my mouth. The key to my penthouse should not have been duplicated without me being notified first.

"Angie toss me them keys. I need to see something. I'mma throw on some sweats and look around for her car."

Chapter 18

She hesitated while she looked at something on the keychain. "What about o'l dirty back there sleeping. If she wake up on some reckless shit, I'm crashing my fist into her face again," she laughed finally tossing the keys.

I looked at what she was staring at, and it was a picture of Stormy and the Diamond King. Which ain't shit. You could tell it was old, because the nigga didn't have no dreads, but the night he died he did.

"What was you staring at this picture so hard for?" I questioned.

"I thought it was my bae, the Diamond King. But he didn't have those pretty long locs, so I tossed you the keys. I was gonna say maybe that hoe ain't lying," Angie admitted.

"Look at this picture again," I said, tossing the keys back to her like Vick in his prime. "As a matter of fact, take a picture of it with your phone, so we can zoom in. I want to make sure what I'm seeing is what I'm seeing. Let me get something to put on, so I can go downstairs and check some shit out. We're gonna tie her up to the bed to make sure she don't move," I conveyed my plan. We both hurried back towards the bathroom.

"Go into my bedroom and grab me those hand cuffs and two belts in that bottom drawer in my closet."

Angie began the scavenger hunt to gather the tools. I removed the drenched and bloodied towel off the face of the troublemaker to check her pulse and make sure she was still breathing. Smack! "Wake up bitch! You ain't dying on me yet."

She opened her eyes, but she didn't speak. I guess she was still groggy from that main event that she lost. I picked her up and placed her on my shoulder and carried her to my bed. My partner in crime looked surprised when she saw us.

"I didn't know you was bringing her in the bedroom. The living room will make it easier for us to keep an eye on her while we find that flash drive," she said.

"Good idea, lil buddy," I joked. I changed the course and went towards the living room. I sat her in a chair while Angie began to lock her down.

"Hey, Anj," I said like a nigga on some fake cool shit."

"Anj? I don't like being called no Anj. Shid Angie is already short enough."

"After tonight you'll be answering to whatever I call you."

"You don't have to threaten me with a good time," she flirted. Angie began stuffing our prisoner's mouth with greasy napkins while I headed to the back and put on something real quick. I scooped up both of her cellphones and headed downstairs while putting in the code and making sure she wasn't lying to me as usual. Both phones unlocked to my birthday, so that part was true. The rain slacked up, but the dampness and the dark grey clouds still prevailed. The air felt good on my skin. Every time the wind blew its soft kisses reminded me that the wind whisperers are here with me. Stormy's car wasn't even out front. There was just the shadow of oxtail stew and small pieces of shattered crockpot left. How the fuck did she even get here? I walked up the block to see if her car was parked on a side street.

"Shit, if I knew she wasn't out front I would have worn a jacket." The drizzle started back up and I put the phones in my pocket and jogged to the corner. The utility men were sitting in their trucks in the process of leaving

127

for the day. I arrived at the corner, and I saw my guy from the Caribbean spot with my food. I waved him down.

"Hey bruddah, what's gwan' on. You out here in dis here weather? Might catch the death out here dress like dem white peoples," he said heavy accent blanketing every word. We shook hands through the open window. "Here get in bruddah. Dis type weather is tricky," he warned unlocking the door.

"What's going on Roots? I'm actually out here looking for a friend of mine's car. You can take the food to my place. Ring the buzzer and she will let you in. Tell Los that I will have something for him to take to the farm for processing later, wrapped and ready by midnight," I informed him.

"Good. I will drop off your meal. Everyting' will be ready. Jus' gimme' call," Roots assured me.

I continued in the same direction for a few minutes longer, and there it was shining like new money. Her tint was super dark, so I couldn't see through the windows. Walked closer and didn't notice anyone inside of the car. I hit the trunk button for shits and giggles. I heard the poppin' sound, but the trunk didn't open. It was stuck. I mashed the button a few more times and it still didn't open. I jerked and pulled the trunk with my left hand freeing it from whatever had it trapped in its claws. The smell was familiar as it blew with the wind in my face. Death was in this trunk and the decedent was Shona Evans. Tortured and mutilated already semi processed for the farm.

"Goddammit!" I said while slamming the trunk. I opened the door and hopped in on some hot shit and drove her car to the back of my building.

"Shit! Los gonna have to definitely make room for at least two now. Those hogs are going to be happy eating these trashy ass bitches." I rambled through her armrest. I didn't find the damn flash drive anywhere, just some fucking trinkets and a lottery ticket with 6673 on it.

Chapter 19

"This bitch was in on killing Church too. I can't wait to get my hands on her triflin' no good ass, I said, rushing out the car damn near forgetting to close the door. "I damn sure don't need that right now. Shid, no murder police, or any other police." I ran through the back entrance and up the stairs. I could smell the oxtails and the frankincense that Roots was wearing.

"Damn why the fuck that nigga scent lingering up here like he camping out?" I can't afford to take another L and get caught slippin'. My 4-5 was stashed behind the fire extinguisher case, so I grabbed it and crept upstairs. My pistol already on go, I came in the door ready to blaze whoever the fuck and whenever the fuck.

"What took you so long, I started eating without you," Angie said, holding the remote.

"Damn, did you find the drive while your greedy ass was sitting around parlaying in this bitch?" I was annoyed by how relaxed she was.

"Yes, I did. For your information, I think I'm finna come on, cause' I'm craving spicy food. That Jamaican habanero sauce was good on my oxtails. They reminded me of the ones my granny used to make," Angie volunteered.

My appetite was shifting like I wasn't hungry no more, but I had to at least taste it, but not before walking over to Stormy's semiconscious body. Smack! "Bitch, you got some explaining to do. Why the fuck you got this lottery ticket and Shona Evans body in your trunk?"

Angie dropped the hot sauce cracking the top, but it didn't spill. I removed the damp napkins from the lying whore's mouth.

"Talk! Now! Lie…. Lie! That's your new name. That's all you do is lie," I taunted her.

"Nigga, fuck you. I ain't telling you shit. I know what the fuck it means when you call down there. She thinks it's food, but I know it's for pet food," Stormy ignored my questions as she threw accusations.

"What the fuck she mean? Am I eating dog food or something? I feel stupid cause the shit good doe," Angie shook her head in disgust.

"Naw crazy! Why the fuck would I feed you dog food?" I asked.

"This bitch is stupid. Craft, after I'm gone you gonna miss me muthafucka. You killed

Church by sending him to play in a league he wasn't built for. I ain't scared to die nigga. I'm dead inside already," our prisoner confessed.

"Well bitch, you finna be dead on the outside too. You was part of all of this from the beginning. You tried to destroy a nigga that would have did anything for you," I admitted.

"You wanted to be quiet with the money. I want to be seen, and I admit I got caught up fuckin with that wild ass young nigga," Stormy said regretfully.

"Where is my ex-stepson? He ain't dead. You niggas trying to sell records. The first rapper resurrected or some shit. That picture on your keychain is a dead giveaway. It wasn't just his haircut. It was your face that still has the scar on your forehead. You got when I first found out about yawl two."

"What the Diamond King is still alive? Shid, where bae?" Angie giggled. Her fascination with that lilnigga was borderline stalkish.

"Shut up Angie!" we both yelled in unison.

"Ya'll ain't got to tell me to shut up. Yawl rude, toxic muthafuckas belong together," the groupie said in-between bites.

"What….what you talkin' about? He dead and gone! You trippin," Stormy said, unconvincingly.

"Hey Stormy. You gonna have to be more convincing than that, but we both know that no matter how hard you try you cannot tell a lie to me without that left eye twitching," I reminded her.

"Your shitty breath got my eye twitching. Both of them," she said.

"Ooh no she didn't!" my sidekick instigated.

"Angie just play the flash drive and quit cosigning from the peanut gallery," I told her immediately.

"You found her body. You know it was Shona," Stormy chimed in ready for her day with the executioner.

"I thought that at first. Her fingertips were slightly burned, but it was most likely from torture, not from setting the fire," I countered on my Columbo shit. I'm betting that it's either you, my ex-stepson or Tags on this video."

Angie chimed in, "I thought it was supposed to be a man. Wouldn't that just leave Tags or Dick? Well, damn. I still can't talk?"

"It ain't Shona, Angie," I interrupted. "She too bougee for that. She is about money and as far as I know she got money without getting her hands dirty. She didn't want it all. She just wanted more than she should have gotten… pure greed. The person or person's responsible was on a power grab, but they wasn't alone. They had inside help. That's where Stormy comes in along with Dick. They had to be the top facilitators in all of this, because they know the most about me. Tags must've double crossed you niggas. That's why you are here trying to pretend to be the key to the resolution when in fact your funky ass is the architect of my attempted ruin."

"Attempted ruin? Nigga, you are finished as of this moment," Stormy spoke as if she had a clever trick up her sleeve.

"Come on out, Roots! I know you are in there." I stuffed the tissue back into the mouth of the traitor, so she couldn't give any warning.

"Roots, I'm not gonna ask you again," I said, warning him this time. "Angie always talking too much when it's a high stress situation. I knew this shit wasn't right. Plus, that oil you are wearing is too heavy. That was the second clue."

He appeared from the back with a clear shot at Angie, but he would have had to turn at an impossible angle to get me from the hallway.

"What happened to legacy Roots…...Don't' you hear me...Legacy!" I shouted barely holding my composure.

"You wanted your legacy to be the greatest and I was offered a better deal bruddah. You blaming me like loyalty is a rule in nature bumble clot. We rude boys…We take what we want."

"You took Church up to the pig farm already. That's why that damn car so clean. In the end, your demise was destined; this isn't luck," I assured him.
The sparks ignited from the barrel as bullets ripped through his face, killing him instantly. He fell dead in the very spot where he stood.

"Angie, your ass took long enough! Good fuckin shot! I guess that pink pistol does get to poppin," I said truly impressed.

"I tried to tell ya. I got that big clit energy!" she said with a straight face.
Angie placed the hot barrel of the gun on Stormy's neck, so she could feel the burn. She squirmed, but she didn't make a sound. I removed the napkins out of her mouth.

"I ain't telling you shit! You gonna have to kill me."

"You ain't in no position to negotiate, so I ain't worried. I'mma let Los know you killed Roots backstabbing ass, and you know that nigga gonna kill your whole family, so bitch get to yapping right fuckin now!" I pressed her even harder. Her eyes began to water. I guess her cold heart was starting to melt a little bit. "That's right momma, daddy, auntie all them muthafuckas dead! The weirdest thing was that nigga was smelling like the same oxtails that I threw out the window. I thought I was trippin off that lil weed. All of this time you ain't been cooking them for me. You been adding something to it and claiming it as your own," I replied in shock. "Stormy, you're just a fraud!"

"You was supposed to have eaten the stew that I added something to today and been incapacitated by the time I came back with the groceries. I anticipated you being more anxious and overwhelmed by the smell," she admitted.

"Trick no good. You spoiled my appetite by showing up here unannounced. Who else is involved? You are going to die for sure at this point. Are you saving the lives of your loved ones? If you feel they aren't worthy of salvation, then let's not waste my time." I broke her cold-hearted ass completely. Her head bowed, and the truth began to spill from the whimper.

"Angie, come over here and sit on the couch. I need to see everybody."
She walked calmly, surprisingly unphased for taking what I assumed to be her first life.

"Who are you working with?" I demanded.

Okay! Okay! I'll tell you. Dick and Tags wanted to replace you, because they had more of a history with each other. They said they didn't agree with the direction you were going with things," she stammered.

"I got that part already. What else? You can cut all of that sniffling out Stormy. We agreed to this ending a long time ago..." I had to pause, because today was our forever, but our forever was necessary.

"I'm sorry it's just that....," she cried.

"Too late for sorry. Spill it!"

"I gotta pee!" she said, trying to distract me.

"Ain't no bathroom breaks. Piss and speak as you sit hoe. You always on the phone when you're in the bathroom anyway."

"Okay! Okay! Tags pulled a move once he realized Dick was going to set him up and replace him with your stepson," Stormy admitted.

"Ex-stepson!" I corrected her ASAP.

"Ex-stepson...He was just a better version of you. Hip, reckless and easy to manipulate with the promises of riches. You were too rigid with principles."

"How can an imitation be better than the original?" I asked.

"He was better for what we needed him for. I started to feel some type of way when I realized that Ice was someone you loved different than you loved me. You put her on a pedestal right next to mines. That big brother cool shit started to change into a level of love. I knew you wanted her to carry your son. It was her womb that you longed for no matter how much you fought it or told me different."

"That's a lie. You ain't even want no kids. You wanted a different life. How can I speak of a legacy without a legacy?" I argued.

"Legacy? You are a murdering muthafucka! Why would I want to bring my son or daughter up into a lifestyle like this," Stormy cried.

"You knew what I was from the beginning. I didn't switch up in the middle like you did. Who the fuck else is it?"

"Los never knew about any of it. His mother got diabete real bad and they had to amputate both of her legs, so Root's been in charge," she explained further.

"I knew Los couldn't've known this shit was way too sloppy. I played chess with that nigga, so I know kinda how he move. But I can't put shit past nobody these days."

"Angie, tell him the rest of the story. Tell him how you was fuckin is ex-stepson as he calls him, and how your brother's change of heart came directly from you and his old lady," Stormy confronted her.

"Bitch what? She lying Craft! I'm the one who signaled that someone was back there."

I switched my attention towards Angie. "What's the rest of the story? If you don't want that son of yours to grow up with only his daddy, then you better start talking!" I yelled.

"I swear on my son, Craft. I had nothing to do with this," Angie whined.

"Hey genius. Who let Roots in the house?" Stormy said, making a valid point, but she was always lying.

"Good point Lie Lie," I said, feeling like I was holding court.

"Of course, I let him in. But he had a gun, so I cooperated. I texted your phone 911. You can check. I thought you read it, and that's why you came in with your gun in your hand," Angie said, attempting to offer reassurance.

The urge to pace came back. I marched back and forth thinking of questions to ask. My mind drew a blank. I grabbed one of Stormy's phones from my pocket to call my phone to see where it was located. Before I could do that, I noticed a text from someone named Main One.

"Who is Main One? I asked Stormy. Before she could respond, I remembered seeing this name somewhere else.

"Angie, who is Main One?" I asked.

"I don't know. Why would I know?" she said, acting jittery.

"Where is your phone?" Naw, don't get up. Where is it?" I asked while pointing the pistol at Angie for the second time today.

"Over there on the counter by the food," she gestured towards the cluttered Island as a reference point. I checked Stormy's restraints. They were still tight. I kept the pistol pointed at Angie.

"What's the code to your phone!" I said, gritting my teeth.

"I don't have a code. It's retina' scan security," Angie spoke while motioning with her hand.

"Gimme that phone. I betchu I crack it with a manual code," Stormy attempted to extended her cuffed and bruised hands.

"I ain't giving you shit!" I refused.

"What's the code Angie?"

"Playboy, you have known the code your whole life," said the troublemaker. Like hot sauce, you put it on everything," Stormy said, antagonizing me. I put 7763 into her phone and it unlocked. I didn't even lift my head to look up at her. I went straight to contacts and there it was, Main One.

"Damn, bitch you too?" I questioned angrily.

"I told you so," Stormy said, givin' it up on the stand like Nino Brown. I walked back to the couch disgusted, but thinking fuck it at the same time. I needed to see her eyes. I stood in front of her, and she began to grin like a snake. Her mask finally came off.

"No shame or nothing bitch?" I asked.

"Shame? Shame for what because I saw myself differently than how you saw me? I always wanted you. I wanted you inside of me.

Being around you in that hospital, I went from wanting to be with you to wanting to beat you. So I went through with the plan."

"Oh, so it's big dick energy! You trying to stand up and piss on walls now?"

"I would still sit and piss, but as The King and not as one of your queens."

"You wasn't there?" I said in disbelief.

"You thought you were planning and scheming, but we planned and schemed on you," she confessed looking away and staring through Stormy.

"You... messy bitch. You had to say something." Angie accused furiously.

"Naw, sit your ass down, Angie. Don't move. Stormy, shut the fuck up. This ain't that."

"I don't know how in the living fuck that we misplaced the flash drive. That messed everything up. The barbecue that you didn't eat had some special sauce on the side that was good for the dippin'. This was the beautiful ending to a tragic love story. You were supposed to clear the path for me as I kept an eye on you," Angie said so truthfully.

"Why didn't you just shoot me if you wanted me dead then?" I wondered out loud.

"Yeah, I should have, but I romanticized your death. I dreamed about you my whole adult life. My girl, she didn't know. She just knew you was coming over and she probably would join us. I was supposed to cook breakfast the next morning. Those lumpy fuckin grits saved your sassy ass life."

"Turtle sent you. I know yawl wasn't going to share the throne with Martha she wasn't going for that."

"Fuck her. My brother was tired of her hoe'n around town embarrassing him," Angie spewed before she was interrupted.

"Angie wasn't supposed to be up here. She was supposed to be at home or somewhere else. I was supposed to get you relaxed and feed you oxtails and have Roots come getchu after you passed out. That fight was real, cause' this bitch fuckin' up my money. This shit was supposed to be simple. Burn down your castle, have you retreat, and checkmate your ass. I just wanted the money. This bitch was too infatuated with the young nigga and her own personal vendetta to see things out," Stormy divulged.

"Hoe please. I would have ground his ass to dust too for me and mines. I didn't mean to stare at that picture so long. We have a similar picture. That's why it caught my eyes."

"Where that lilnigga hiding at?" The room went silent. No one spoke up. "Shid don't ya'll speak at once, but somebody betta' say something and I mean right muthafuckan now!" I demanded with emphasis.

"I didn't know that wasn't my part and at this point I ain't got no reason to lie to you nigga." Crack! Was the sound the pistol made as I drummed Angie in the head with the butt of my gun.

"OWWW!" she grimaced loudly. "Nigga, you wasn't the only one dying tonight. What you thought Ice wouldn't be a bargaining chip. She is spoils of war. Tags probably up there cutting out her fucking tongue as we speak."

"Bitch, you bluffin.' She's guarded real tight. Ice ain't even at the hospital no more. I had her moved to an undisclosed location. I always had my antennas up with you, because of who your brother is. At this point, I don't need either one of you bitches. I know who is left and I know how I'm going to get them. You can't checkmate the Kingmaker."

Angie bull rushed me to try to get my gun and overpower me. I sidestepped her and damn near tripped over Roots' body. Stormy rocked her chair and fell over damn near taking out my legs. During the confusion, Angie went for her pink pistol with nothing to lose. She started shooting wildly and emptied her clip. My heart was beating out of my chest. I was still alive not hit, and her pistol was out of bullets. She threw the gun at me and hit the wall. In the final act, she grabbed a knife and rushed me once more. But this time was her last time. My gun went off striking her twice in her chest. Her lifeless body fell and so did the knife.

"Man, I need to learn how to pick better women," I said while grabbing my knee.

"Hey Stormy. Here, let me give you your final meal." I picked up a big saucy oxtail that Roots brought over and stuffed it in her mouth.

"Naw, bitch. Don't spit. Be a good girl and swallow. It was either you alone or you, and everything you love." She put up some resistance for a minute before finally accepting her fate. Her mouth completely wrapped in duct tape only left her nose partially exposed, so she could die slowly. My mission wasn't complete. There were a few people left. Stormy's and Angie's phones both started buzzing at the same time. I picked them both up, and it was a message from Main One.

Main One:
7:45 p.m.
Martha and Turtle were both found in their homes dead.

Chapter 20

BREAKING NEWS: "Reporting to you live on the scene of a police chase and shootout on I-75 south that resulted in multi vehicle pileup.

A car carrying semi-truck overturned bursting into flames. The driver is believed to be Tommy "Tags" Onnetta. Early reports are stating that Mr. Onnetta was under investigation for being the ringleader of an elaborate scheme to steal over $100 million from taxpayers.

A strange smell permeates the air along with diesel fuel. A special hazmat team is on the scene combatting the fire. There are several fatalities being reported including some law enforcement. Over my left shoulder, you can see the SWAT team in tactical gear along with several responding officers from districts throughout the county. Directly to the north, you can see many vehicles engulfed in flames.

We'll keep you updated as the news breaks.

www.ingramcontent.com/pod-product-compliance
Lightning Source LLC
Chambersburg PA
CBHW060121260626
47160CB00005B/1969